GHOST IN THE SHELL

Also available from Titan Books

The Art of Ghost in the Shell

GHOST  IN THE SHELL

THE OFFICIAL
MOVIE NOVELIZATION

BASED ON THE COMIC *THE GHOST IN THE SHELL*
BY SHIROW MASAMUNE
SCREENPLAY BY JAMIE MOSS AND WILLIAM WHEELER
AND EHREN KRUGER
DIRECTED BY RUPERT SANDERS
NOVELIZATION BY JAMES SWALLOW
AND ABBIE BERNSTEIN

TITAN BOOKS

Ghost in the Shell: The Official Movie Novelization
Print edition ISBN: 9781785657528
E-book edition ISBN: 9781785657535

Published by Titan Books
A division of Titan Publishing Group Ltd
144 Southwark Street, London SE1 0UP

First edition: September 2017
1 3 5 7 9 10 8 6 4 2

A CIP catalogue record for this title is available from the British Library.

Printed and bound by CPI Group (UK) Ltd, Croydon, CR0 4YY

Did you enjoy this book? We love to hear from our readers. Please email us at readerfeedback@titanemail.com or write to us at Reader Feedback at the above address.

To receive advance information, news, competitions, and exclusive offers online, please sign up for the Titan newsletter on our website: **www.titanbooks.com**

GHOST IN THE SHELL

FOR TOREN SMITH

In the future, the line between human and machine is disappearing. Advancements in technology allow humans to enhance themselves with cybernetic parts.

Hanka Robotics, funded by the government, is developing a military operative that will blur the line even further. By transplanting a human brain into a fully synthetic body, they will combine the strongest attributes of human and robot.

PROLOGUE

A NEW SHELL

Who am I?

The question terrified her. It made all the rest of her confusion trivial. She did not know where she was, how she had gotten here, what had happened before.

She also knew that she was being moved, not under her own power. She was being propelled steadily forward. The movement was smooth, and she could see what was above her, so she must be on her back. She could not even tell whether she was in pain. *Something* was surely wrong with her. She was in a white long-sleeved robe made of some light fabric that didn't keep the cold out. She felt like she could not sit up, could not swing her legs. And her breathing wasn't normal. There was some sort of mask over her nose and mouth. The air circulating through it didn't taste right.

There were people around her, on both sides and

running along after, all of them dressed in medical gloves, hoods, and protective masks, all colored bright arterial red. As a group, the med team looked like a swarm of red corpuscles, flowing through a vein made of white industrial tile. They all had visors on, each one running a steady stream of holographic data before the medics' eyes.

The medical team also wore hard black semi-vests over their coats, all with a yellow Hanka logo on the back. One man, not part of the team, was wearing a dark suit. He stood to the side, letting the others rush past.

Had she been in an accident? She couldn't remember. She managed to get up one hand to pull her mask off, but a red-gloved hand grasped her wrist and put it down on the gurney, and she didn't have the strength to raise it a second time. There was something made of plastic circling her wrist, though she couldn't bring it up to where she could see it. The object was a clear wristband with a yellow tag that that read PROJECT 2751.

A woman's voice calmly announced over the PA system, "Oxygen levels are dropping." And indeed, she was having trouble breathing. What was wrong? Was she dying? She was aware of her gurney passing through an archway and stopping inside a room.

"Brain function normal," said the woman over the PA system.

So perhaps she didn't have brain damage. But

then why wouldn't any clear memories come to her?

And then the room dimmed and thought ceased, so she did not hear the next announcement over the PA system. "Cerebral salvage ready to proceed."

In the operating room, technology reigned supreme. Each piece of cybernetic equipment, gleaming-edged tools and lasers too thin for eyes to track and translucent strands of delicate-looking but powerful transmitters, all moved without the aid of human hands around the young woman, preparing her for the upcoming procedure.

Project 2571's scalp was peeled back cleanly, the skull opened and the brain removed, but the only humans at work were several rooms away, programming the surgical devices moving in a complicated ballet of exacting incisions and removal.

The subject's human brain, gold techno-enhancements faintly visible against the pink organic matter, was contained cleanly in a black synthetic brain case, which was stamped with the Hanka logo, even though this would not be seen by anyone unless the project terminated. When the brain had been temporarily stabilized and the rest of the associated organic matter had been disposed of, the PA system again broadcast updates of the procedure. "Robotic skeleton prepared and waiting for brain insertion. Initiate Project Two-Five-Seven-One."

Imagine a synthesis of both things, of mechanism and human. Call it *cyborg*. A blending of organic intellect and mechanical perfection, biology's ultimate living computer encased within technology's ultimate physical form. Mind and machine in perfect harmony.

In the Hanka Robotics Corporation, there was a chamber known as the Shelling Room. No humans ever entered it. Every action was completed with rote perfection by synthetic intelligences and flawless computer programs. What took place within the space was of such incredible complexity that a mere human could not hope to control it. Only the machines could truly birth another of their kind. Only they were able to assemble the mechanism with infinite precision and unerring patience.

Deep in a tank of dark liquid, a vertical humanoid skeleton, painstakingly constructed by Hanka scientists, gleamed in the low light. Over the skeletal form made of titanium alloy and hyper-density polymers, artificial organs were placed, gathered in such a way that their functions could both emulate and exceed those of a human. Across the assemblage, a complex web of thread-thin mech-nerves were overlaid and twinned with myomer muscle groups, vat-grown in zero-gravity. Tendrils of composite organic and synthetic materials reached up from the skeleton to connect with compatible translucent filaments reaching down from the incoming brain case.

The mecha-composite slowly began to resemble something human, something feminine, but only in the most abstract sense. It was a diagram from an anatomy book, a skinless horror.

The artificial shell was suspended, adrift and without life or mind. The skull—a layered device, petal upon petal of armored metal and electroactive polymer—unfastened gently. A clockwork action, a music box opening, the petals peeled back until the empty void within was fully revealed.

Cables guided Project 2571's human brain into this new housing. The shroud of meat and bone that it had animated was now gone. The pink matter was swallowed whole by the artificial cranium.

When the cables had released the brain case, the skull closed and the entire body was released to float downward to the bottom of the tank. From inside the surface of the brain case, innumerable fiber-optic tendrils unfurled and quested forth to pierce the protective sack. Connections fused into the biological tissue, building unique neural linkages and bridging the gap between the flesh and the metal. The fibers merged themselves with the dendrites and synapses of the living cerebellum. The interface was completed.

The surgery could have taken place in total darkness, but the scientists felt the need to observe, making sure it was all going as planned. A few red lights within the tank provided illumination for those watching through the viewing portals.

The flow of conductive liquid in the tank was now orchestrated to turn the body onto its back. The pressure pushed the human-shaped form into another tank, this one lit red. Here it was coated with a white substance, a quarter-inch-thick layer of a white cellular/plastic compound that set over the entire body, allowing the layers of skin and flesh and electronics to fuse undisturbed. Each millimeter contained microscopic biomechanical circuitry that would enable the brain and its host to complete tasks that neither machinery nor humanity on its own could ever achieve. Then the body floated upward in the chamber, gravity turned off so there was no point of contact between the floor and the forming epidermis.

Once the process was complete, the white compound broke up in a multitude of pieces that fluttered away like small, startled birds to reveal the entity beneath. A cyber-mech body, fully artificial in every way, but operated by a thinking, feeling, *living* human mind. There were markings across the new body, like pieces of a jigsaw puzzle, but these would soon become almost undetectable.

While it was in no way the purpose of the project, most observers would have agreed that 2571 was beautiful. Her features were elfin and delicate in some ways, cold and inviolate in others. She had wide-set eyes, a bow-shaped mouth, breasts that tapered to a firm waist and long, powerful legs. Her skin was pale, which made for a dramatic contrast with her jet-black hair, which came to just below her earlobes.

She had yet to open her new, augmented eyes,

looking like a porcelain statue, the lines in the dermal plates that formed her cheeks and her brow barely visible. They faded by the moment as her skin grew more real, more human in tone. Soon she would be indistinguishable from the organic. At least, outwardly, except for the four dark quik-ports in the back of her neck, but so many people had those these days that the ports simply made her look like a functioning member of society. Her form was covered by a transparent sheet, which in turn was covered by the glowing red of the scan-grid running through the conductive material.

Then she was awake again, but just as confused as she had been before. She saw rapidly changing colors— white, yellow, orange, blue—and her fingers trembled. She knew she was moving them, but couldn't feel anything around them. Not comfort, not warmth, not cold, not... anything. Was this normal? All she could remember was... water. She had been sinking in water, it had been cold... A voice spoke. Its owner sounded kind. "Now your eyes are going to open."

Only then did she realize her eyes were closed. She opened them and she could see, but there was still no sensation. It was disturbing.

She was in what looked like a hospital operating room, lying supine on an exam table that was lit from within. A very bright light was directly above her. The doctor who'd spoken now pulled back the sheet. "There. You're safe now." The woman, dressed in bright red scrubs, had warm brown eyes and a welcoming smile.

She realized that there were restraints on her upper arms, keeping her from sitting up. Something was plugged into her neck. And she was having trouble breathing. There was no feeling of air going in, of lungs holding oxygen, of expelling air. She gasped.

"It's okay," the doctor maintained. "Just breathe."

She couldn't stop gasping, hearing how harsh it sounded and still feeling nothing. The doctor repeated, "Just breathe."

She tried to stop fighting her own panic. Her gasps began to subside into raspy inhalations and exhalations.

"Breathe," the doctor said once more.

The rasps became shaky breaths.

The doctor smiled. "Good," she said, her voice soft. "That's good. Hello, Mira." The doctor put a red-gloved hand on the edge of the exam table, as if to demonstrate that she was right here, ready to help if needed.

Mira, she thought. *That's my name.* It sounded unfamiliar to her, but nothing else seemed familiar, either. Certainly this room wasn't. And had she ever met this doctor before?

Maybe not, because the doctor felt the need to introduce herself. "I'm Dr. Ouelet."

Mira focused on the woman. She was perhaps about fifty, with a sympathy in her dark eyes that matched her voice. "Do you remember anything about the attack?"

An attack? That would explain why she was in a hospital. But Mira didn't remember. "What happened?" Then she recalled the water, floating downward in the darkness. She trembled. "I was... I was drowning." The memory hit her then, with force—loss of control, terror, a wave over her head. "There's water!" She gulped reflexively.

"That's right," Dr. Ouelet said. "You were on a boat. A refugee boat."

In Mira's mind, the images formed. She was on a boat with her family, crammed together with many other families. She recalled the sounds—sharp voices arguing, someone laughing, a child crying—and the smell of too many people too long unwashed sharing too small a space. Then there had been a flash, and flames, and a murderous metal scream as the deck ruptured and tilted and water was everywhere...

"It was sunk by terrorists," Dr. Ouelet explained. The water had been icy, and Mira had been cut by splintering wood. But now she couldn't feel the places where she had been cut, or the temperature in the hospital room, or her fingers and toes, or her breath. It was horrible. "Why can't I feel my body?"

Dr. Ouelet's voice remained gentle. She gave an encouraging smile, as though Mira shouldn't be made afraid by what she said next. "Mira, your body was damaged. We couldn't save it."

That made no sense. An arm, a leg, an eye could be lost. But Mira couldn't be lying here, listening to the doctor, without... But she couldn't feel anything. Not cold air on her face, not the examination table underneath her. She could not feel her lungs, or the pulse of her heart. She gasped and began to tremble.

Dr. Ouelet continued her soft, terrible explanation. "Only your brain survived. We made you a new body. A synthetic shell." Then she smiled and nodded, as if what she was saying was meant to be reassuring. "But your mind, your soul... your 'ghost'..." The doctor lowered her voice to a whisper, as though making it seem like a secret should ease Mira's fears. "It's still in there."

Mira tried to follow what the doctor was saying. She looked around, but there were no clues in this sterile room. Her memories were incoherent. She couldn't remember her family, not really, not why they'd been on the boat or where they had come from, but she remembered being human, being at home in her own skin. This was... this was not...

The synthetic shell, as the doctor called it, did take breaths, but it seemed to need something from Mira to do it properly, and all at once she couldn't. She began hiccupping uncontrollably, and as she couldn't catch her breath, she began shaking, until the shakes became convulsions and her back slammed against the examination table.

Dr. Ouelet stepped back from Mira and gestured

to two waiting nurses. "Please." The nurses stepped forward, awaiting instruction. "Sedate her."

The more junior nurse hesitated to use a syringe on a patient who was moving so unpredictably, but the senior nurse commanded, "Put it in her arm. Now."

The junior nurse succeeded in administering the sedative into Mira without having the needle snap off in the patient's jerking arm. The drug took effect almost at once, and Mira's convulsions subsided into shakes, her gasps into small, inarticulate sounds.

Once it was clear that Mira was in no danger, Dr. Ouelet left the operating room and stepped into her office, which was just on the other side of a wide observation window that ran almost the length of the connecting wall. She emitted a tense sigh, not looking forward to the conversation she was obliged to have with the man who was waiting for her. It was the same man who had been in the corridor when the team had wheeled Project 2571 in for the extraction surgery.

Hanka's chief executive officer Leslie Cutter was in his forties, with dark hair swept back from his forehead. His black suit was almost as expensive as the yellow ocular implant in his right eye and the dark neural enhancer visible in his left temple. In practical terms, the suit had cost him more; as head of Hanka Robotics, he hadn't had to pay anything for his cyber-enhancements. "Will it work?" he asked Ouelet.

"Absolutely." Ouelet was proud of her own work,

but also proud of how well Mira had withstood the test of having her essence put into its new shell. "She's a miracle." Guessing what Cutter was thinking, Ouelet continued, "A machine can't lead, it can only follow orders. A machine can't imagine, or care, or intuit. But as a human mind in a cybernetic frame, Mira can do all those things... and more." She momentarily looked away from her visitor to study the holographic blue stream of data scrolling down over the window.

When Cutter spoke again, it was clear to Ouelet that he understood the operation was a success—and comprehended almost none of its implications. "The first of her kind. She will join Section Nine as soon as she is operational."

Ouelet tried hard to keep hold of her temper. She and her team had succeeded in creating a new life form, and Cutter simply saw Mira as a tool for law enforcement. "Please, please don't do that. You're reducing a complex human to a machine."

"I don't think of her as a machine." Cutter's voice was bland as he dismissed Ouelet's concerns. "She's a weapon. And the future of my company."

Cutter turned and left. Ouelet turned to look through the observation window at the examining room beyond. Mira was now sleeping peacefully.

1

SOLID STATE

A year later, nothing and everything was new in New Port City. As its name suggested, the place was a major shipping destination, with a heavily trafficked harbor. It was also a hub of international industry, a magnet for worldwide corporate dealings.

The night sky above was a dark cowl of heavy cloud, dense with unspent rain, looming over myriad steel and glass skyscrapers that reached toward it like the fingers of some giant machine.

Due to the peculiarities of the city's microclimate, it rained here often, but tonight the weather-modification technology kept the downpour in check. Traffic ran on multiple levels through downtown, with steel arches placed over each road at regular intervals both to hold up the infrastructure and to remind distracted drivers of the lane parameters. Green and red shimmering holographic signals pointed out on-ramps and off-ramps to the motorists. Packed in atop one another, the citizens ebbed and flowed through the avenues of the downtown core in pulses, mimicking the patterns of electrons through some vast circuit diagram. From high above, it was impossible to discern individual figures on the walkways or in the vehicles. There was only the flow of light and color, the constant motion. The city-as-machine, endlessly running.

The sky, though, was full. Some things in it were simply for civic beautification, like the holograms of shimmering, glittering spheres that suggested New Port City was a place of glamour and joy. But most of the skyline was dedicated to commerce. Advertising was everywhere, on the sides of buildings and floating free in the air. Holograms, many of them towering higher than the city's forest of skyscrapers, hawked everything imaginable, everywhere the eye could see, in every color of the spectrum. Solograms—holograms that appeared to be solid—proliferated as well. The audio for the ads was easily accessed on a variety of phone apps or cyber-augmented hearing channels within the ear, for those who were interested.

One floating billboard crossed the sky, while a male announcer on the audio declared, "Introducing Bridgeworks from Lippastrift Technologies, the first artificially created memory enhancement..."

The hologram competed for airspace and attention with many others. One simply advertised something called "Locus Slocus." Another promoted "virtu-learning" from Hanka Robotics. In another a female announcer promised, "Sirenum's training protocol is the fastest and most efficient way to develop the abilities you've always wanted."

A fifth holographic billboard showed a man with a techno-enhanced hand. A male voice enthused, "Stronger than ever. Experience your power with PneumaGrip." A sixth billboard had a contrasting style, as it was from law enforcement rather than a corporate sales division. Part of it read, in huge letters, "CYBER CRIME IS PUNISHED SEVERELY." For those still unclear on the concept, the audio warned, "Cyber crime is a type-one offense. Minimum punishment: fifteen years in prison."

Hanka Robotics, arguably the world's largest corporation, probably didn't need to advertise itself. Then again, perhaps its prominence was due in part to its relentless self-promotion. It had yet another hologram commercial winding through New Port City airspace: "Protect your life essence, with virtu-lock technology. Hanka Robotics guarantees personal safety and integrity against outside threats." With so many readily available bodily implants, this was a danger facing most ordinary consumers.

More ads, some aggressive like the fifty-foot geisha advertising a nightclub, some subtler, like the zeppelin-sized solographic koi that swam between buildings, all clamored for attention in a variety of languages—English, Japanese, Cantonese, Arabic and more—as tuners in cars and radios and implants changed channels.

On a restricted channel, heard only by the city's law enforcement personnel, one voice came through unopposed. "All patrolling air units be advised. Possible cyber-crime activity in the vicinity. Airspace in all adjoining areas to be locked down. Section Nine is currently on site. Repeat: All patrolling air units be advised. Possible cyber-crime activity—" the voice faded a little, its wavelength compromised by the uncountable others, "—in the vicinity. All airspace..."

With the enormous, vividly colored images moving everywhere, few people would even try to look through and past them to anything more solid. It would take both augmented optics and tactical knowledge to see a single figure, perched on a rooftop.

The Major—this was how she thought of herself now; only Ouelet called her Mira—blinked. She stood near the edge of the towering building. Her visor was pushed up on her forehead as she looked down and across the street through the ocular implants that the rest of the world saw as lovely, but normal, green eyes. The edges of her long matte-black coat to flapped against her legs in the wind.

Across the street from the Major, the Maciej Hotel was one of the city's biggest towers, a jagged shard of reflective emerald and spun-lattice lunar steel that reached a dizzying one hundred floors high.

Every level was an exercise in opulent luxury, with dozens of suites and bespoke rooms assembled atop each other to appeal to the richest men and women visiting the city, or even richer locals looking to impress someone.

The Major looked down into the sheer drop between her position and the hotel opposite. The wind toyed with her, threatening to push her over the edge and into the gulf. She imagined the fall; the thought held no fear. The solograms briefly won her notice, each one claiming to offer the key to a better future through cybernetic improvement. The Major looked away from the advertisements and down at her gloved hands, pondering whether cybernetic enhancement, planned and voluntary, unlike her own, really did make people's lives better. She saw herself reflected in the ideal identity the corporations were promoting. Her young face framed by short dark hair, with its deep eyes and old soul beneath. The body of an athlete all spare lines, lean and flawless. And within that shell—

"This is Major. I'm on site." She didn't need to speak, or even subvocalize her response; the mind-comms link implanted in her neck gave her a kind of machine-telepathy that was routed directly back to Chief Aramaki at headquarters, and to the rest of her tactical team looped into the encrypted network. She could almost sense them out there in the darkness, faint phantom presences that existed

just beyond the limits of her perception.

"*Awaiting instructions.*"

"*Review and report.*" The dour, resonant voice seemed to be conjured out of the air itself, perfectly clear despite the moaning winds across the Maciej's rooftop.

The chief's words formed directly in the Major's auditory nerve matrix, rendered silent and encrypted by one of the many neural modules beneath the surface of her skin. Even through the non-vocal link, the voice carried the same cadence as ever; every word precise, every sentence cut exactly to length. In all her time serving under Daisuke Aramaki's command as a field operative for the Public Security Section Nine counter-terrorism unit, the Major had rarely heard the steely old man raise his voice. There had never been the need. She'd also never heard him speak anything other than Japanese, either aloud or through the comms. He did not require that others respond to him in Japanese, only that he be understood in his own words. This was not an issue for the Major. She couldn't remember whether the language was something she already knew in her previous life or had been added to her linguistic skills as part of a cyber implant, but her Japanese was as flawless as her English.

Sixty floors below, a geisha bot in a floor-length red

kimono, bound by a golden sash, made her way down one of the many corridors of the luxury Maciej Hotel. The floor was lit from beneath, a pattern of white rectangles outlined in black. One wall was covered in a curtain with a gold and black motif of water.

The geisha bot swayed gracefully as she moved. Like the décor, her appearance was meant to conjure the Japan of centuries past, but she was not meant to be mistaken for a human. Her faceplate was a painted feminine mask, glossy milk white with a perfect circle of pink that encompassed the area between her mid-forehead and lower lip. Darker pink eyebrows were painted at the top of the circle, and a small vertical rectangle of crimson marked the exact center of her mouth. Her hair was black lacquer, fanned out in the back with one section that rose up and two that framed her face. Her eyes were black and held no expression.

The geisha bot entered the wide space of a banquet room. This, too, was in the style of old Japan. Here, another geisha bot played the strings of a quiet samisen, picking out a melancholy, traditional tune, long alabaster fingers never missing a single motion as they travelled up and down the neck of the stringed instrument. Her head turned this way and that. She and the other geisha bots in service, all identical in form, had variations in the pink patterns on their masks, but all were clad in black kimonos—except for the one in red who had just arrived.

Human hostesses would have been completely superfluous here, as no one in the room would have cared to interact with them in any case. Bots not only suited the purpose, but the theme of the gathering; after all, the meeting in the banquet room was all about tech.

The executives of Hanka in their expensive suits and the delegates from the West African Federation in their brightly hued robes sat cross-legged on floor mats on either side of a long, low wooden table. They laughed and conversed, eating their expensive meal with chopsticks as the synthetic servants walked among them, topping up their sake and tea bowls from cast-iron kettles.

The red-clad geisha sat down behind Dr. Paul Osmond. He took no notice of her. Lean and gravel-voiced, Osmond was the head of Hanka's robotics division, far too preoccupied to even look round as he held up his bowl for a refill. His dark silk jacket was a trifle too large; the stress of trying to get this deal in place had taken its toll on his sleep and appetite. Osmond kept his attention fixed on the visitors he had worked so very hard to bring here. The geisha drifted away and he took a sip of sake, savoring the bitter taste, and continued his conversation. "I'm human, I'm flawed," Osmond confessed to the assemblage. "But I embrace change... and enhancement. Now there's nothing I can't do. Nothing... nothing I can't know. Nothing I can't be."

Osmond turned purposefully to the West African Federation's president. The man's shaved head and unlined face, framed by a neat beard, made his age difficult to judge. The president's turquoise blue and saffron robes suggested that he was open to colorful possibilities; the dark implants at both temples proclaimed that the man was definitely in favor of cyber-enhancement; the fragrant, half-smoked cigar he gestured with in his right hand said he was a connoisseur of fine things.

Osmond took all of these as good signs. "I want you to listen to something," he told the president.

Pressing a thumb-pad that shone with golden light, Osmond sent impulses through the president's transparent cyber-enhancement lines, which lit up with a series of blue flashes as information was transmitted directly into his brain.

The president closed his eyes to concentrate, smiling at what he heard. A little English girl sang a few bars from a classic French song. *"Au clair de la lune/Mon ami Pierrot..."*

"That's my four-year-old daughter," Osmond explained. "In the time it took her to sing that lullaby, she learned to speak fluent French."

The president opened his eyes and leant forward, smiling at Osmond. Osmond felt his confidence increase. He tried to keep his mind on the business at hand, instead of thinking ahead to the promotion this contract would net him, and of the salary bump that would come with it.

The Major heard Osmond trying to be cool and conversational through an echo box, a type of cavity resonator used to test and adjust radar equipment by bouncing a signal between the transmitter and the receiver. "Did you know that song was the earliest known recording?"

The Major's mental databases immediately referred her to what was being referenced—a voice singing "Au Clair de la Lune" had been made on a phonautograph, the earliest known device for recording sound, in 1860, by Édouard-Léon Scott de Martinville. *What* she was hearing, however, concerned her far less than *how* she was hearing it. The presence of the device was unexpected, and therefore suspicious.

"*There's an echo box*," she told Aramaki over the comms. The Major opened her kit. One end of the serpentine zeta-cable within presented six jacks that snapped smartly into sockets on the base of the echo box, and the other spooled around her wrist, almost as if it were alive. She took it between her fingers and reached up to the back of her neck, folding away her hair to access her quik-ports. The zeta-cable, made from a smart polymer configured for ultra-high density data transfer, whispered into her dermal receiver ports and clicked home with a soft sigh.

She stiffened slightly as her neural software made the interface with the echo box and the Maciej Hotel's security network. Military-grade digital incursion programs made short work of the rudimentary countermeasures protecting the illegal tech.

The president of the West African Federation apparently had the same information about the recording as the Major did. She heard him say, "Édouard-Léon Scott de Martinville…"

Computer information was being moved across a network, the Major concluded, and it wasn't her team. "*Someone's scanning data traffic,*" she reported.

Aramaki's command came back over the comm. "*Trace where it's transmitting.*"

. The Major wanted to visually identify the conversation she overheard through the echo box. "*Let's see who's worth this kind of surveillance.*" She knew the comms would carry her words to the rest of Section Nine. She lowered her virtual reality headset and focused it on the Maciej Hotel. Within milliseconds, the Major was seeing the live feeds from the Maciej's embedded cameras that the device had intercepted. This in turn allowed her to scan through every room in the hotel, private or public, searching for where the unit was transmitting. "*Accessing hotel security network.*"

Snatches of distorted discussion—laughter, arguments, legalese, appreciations of cuisine—came through the Major's VR headset. The VR also provided images, tracings of furniture and architectural constructions and human heat signatures. These didn't provide tremendous detail, but the Major could see enough to know that she didn't detect anyone doing anything that seemed like it would attract a voyeur, much less the planting of malicious spy equipment.

As her superior, Aramaki had access to current intelligence on the hotel that the Major did not; the chief could more easily find out where any important meetings might be occurring on the premises, so that he could just tell the Major and end her room-by-room search. "*What are you seeing, sir?*" she asked into the comm. "*I've got a lotta hotel to scan.*"

A hologram of the Maciej Hotel in glowing gold outline appeared on Aramaki's desk. Registry lists scrolled beside the visual. The chief looked through them for possible locations. One immediately stood out. "*There is a banquet room reserved for the President of the African Federation,*" he told the Major. "*Dr. Osmond is hosting for Hanka Robotics.*"

The Major adjusted her VR headset so that she could see into the banquet room. Her first impression was that it looked much like any other high-end business gathering being conducted over dinner. She caught the end of a sentence in Osmond's English accent as he said, "...at a time."

"*Got it,*" the Major said on her comm. As she zoomed in, the visuals gained color and solidity, until she could see clear facial features and body language. She honed in on Osmond, who was identified by a holographic tag in her vision. "*Forty-third floor.*"

She looked across the table, and saw the man her holographic readout identified as "President of West African Federation." She thought rapidly of what all of this might mean, barely hearing the president as he articulated what he knew for Osmond's benefit. "The early technology utilized the human body..."

In fact, the inventor Alexander Graham Bell had used preserved parts of the ears of human cadavers in his early experiments with the phonoautograph, which made it a very early ancestor of the bio-tech that was now embodied by the Major. On another, less pressing occasion, such history might have intrigued her. Now, though, the Major sensed impending disaster. "*Someone contact the president's staff,*" she said, her urgency clear over the comms. "*Someone's watching him.*"

Neither the president nor the people in the room with him were aware of this. The president was simply focused on the matters at hand. "Dr. Osmond... what is it you want from us?"

"I think it's more about what Hanka Robotics can do for *you*," Osmond replied. That got him a few appreciative murmurs from some of the African leader's retinue. He was winning them over. It would just take one last push to bring it home, and then he would walk out of here with the most lucrative contract his employers had seen in decades. "Seventy-three percent of this world has... woken up to the age of cyber-enhancement. You really want to be left behind?"

The president smiled, wondering if his sentiments would have any impact on the other man, whose belief in mechanization was absolute. "My people embrace cyber-enhancement, as do I." He didn't really need to state this; tech augmentation was clearly visible somewhere on every member of the delegation. "But there's no one who really understands the risk… to individuality, identity… messing with the human soul."

Now that she had a probable target, the Major brought up everything she could reach on the security network, assembling a patchwork of images and data streams on her VR glasses. She captured the video from every camera on the forty-third level, the readouts of every fire alarm, thermostat and air quality monitor, all of it unfolding before her.

When the secure elevator opened at the end of the hallway outside the banquet suite, the Major felt it like the distant tensing of a muscle. *That's not right.* According to the Maciej's security server, the express and local elevators to the forty-third floor had been locked off for the duration of the meeting, deactivated for all but the direst of emergency circumstances.

Six Asian men in identical dark suits of corporate cut, carrying identical briefcases, all exited the elevator in swift order and approached the closed doors to the banquet room. They were differentiated mainly by the style of VR glasses they wore and the placement of their facial scars.

The two grey-suited Hanka security bots

standing guard outside the banquet room looked human. One prepared to stop the unfamiliar men, saying, "Gentlemen, excuse me, I think you have the wrong—" But before the bot could finish the lead stranger shot both bots down, leaving them sparking and inoperative. The faceplate of one slid upward, revealing a black skull casing and a glowing red light that dimmed as the guard's functions ceased.

The Major felt a surge of an adrenaline-analogue flood through her, but she was controlled as she spoke into her comm. *"Hallway. Six men. Shots fired. Section Nine ETA?"*

She listened for the sound of police sirens, her aural software picking out the faint skirl on the breeze wafting upward. Sergeant Batou was usually her backup in these situations, but the mission brief hadn't shown a need for him tonight.

This meant the stocky Scandinavian was driving a Section Nine jeepney as fast as he could toward the Major's position. With him were Borma, Togusa, Ishikawa, Saito, and Ladriya. Section Nine was the most highly skilled and lethal anti-cyber-terrorism squad in the district, perhaps the country. But, right now, Batou felt as though they might as well be traffic cops. The Major needed them, and here they were, nowhere near in position and still on the road. Their intelligence profile for this operation had been low-threat with a clear objective, to follow up on intel chatter about a possible data intrusion at the Maciej, but he thought that was no excuse. "*Two minutes out, Major.*"

"*Too long,*" the Major said into the comms. "*I'm goin' in.*" She pulled the VR headset's cable from her cyber-enhanced neck ports, ending the transmission of the scan to Aramaki.

"*Hold!*" Aramaki shouted into the comm, but the Major was no longer listening.

Within the corridor of the Maciej Hotel, the six assassins continued forward, all pressing the catches on their briefcases at the same time. The cases dropped to the floor, leaving each of the men holding a stubby machine gun.

With a flick of her wrist, the Major cast off her black coat, revealing a pale combat thermoptic bodysuit beneath. Silk-thin, the material was made of an ultra-light compound that could turn a blade or low-caliber round at close range. But this was not the material's greatest advantage. When inactive, the thermoptic suit looked white, with a jigsaw, fish-scale pattern connecting its sections. Activated, the thermoptics made the suit and its wearer virtually invisible; someone looking for it might see a rippling shape in the air, something that looked like clear glass shimmering through water, but no more than that.

"*Major, stop!*" Aramaki commanded, but he could not hear her presence on the comms. She had disabled hers, probably so that she wouldn't hear any more direct orders from him that countered her own perceptions about what she should do next. Aramaki's mouth tightened. The Major was a superb agent, but there was such a thing as taking too much initiative in the name of duty.

On the rooftop, the Major took a pistol out of the holster built into the side of her uniform. She cocked the weapon.

In the banquet room, Dr. Osmond felt in danger. His cherished plan was being demolished, bit by bit, with every word his hoped-for client uttered. "I've heard this speech before," the president declared, "from your competitors."

The geisha in the red kimono poured more sake into Osmond's cup. The president gestured at the beverage.

Osmond felt something wet on his hand and looked down to see the sake had filled the bowl and was now overflowing, streaming over the sides and spilling on to the lacquered table beneath. "What are you doing?" the doctor demanded of the artificial geisha. It continued to pour as if his cup was still empty, and Osmond saw the president push back in his seat, suddenly dismayed.

"And now, Hanka Robotics serves it with milky sake," the president finished, as though the malfunctioning geisha was making his point for him.

Osmond colored, his fury building. He had come too far to have this all ruined because of some mechanical glitch. Maintenance had assured him all the bioroids at the hotel had been in perfect working order. The geisha began to blink rapidly, and then its jet-black doll's eyes refocused on his face. "Hey!" he snapped, aiming a finger at the errant machine. "Hey, hey, hey!"

The machine ignored him and Osmond finally put his hand over the cup to stop the overflow.

The geisha's reaction was as fast as a striking cobra. Her pale white hand shot out and grabbed Osmond's finger, bending it the wrong way against the joint with a percussive crack of snapping bone. He let out a high-pitched scream as the president and his retinue fell back, and the other Hanka execs scattered in surprise. Pain lanced through his arm and Osmond desperately tried to extract himself from the geisha's grasp. He was having difficulty adjusting to the sudden change in his predicament. Just a few seconds ago he had been worried about losing the account and now it seemed that he might be about to lose much more.

The president reacted to the geisha's actions with fear, tinged by righteous indignation. "This is what I'm talking about."

Osmond might have replied, but the geisha struck him across the head with the sake pot and spun him around. He screamed again.

"Whoa!" the president yelled. Some of the banquet guests began to shout and rise to their feet in confused panic; others simply asked what was happening.

Dazed and half-blinded, Osmond felt the synthetic

pull him into a chokehold and tighten its grip on his neck. He gasped for air as his vision swam. The three other geisha bots took hold of other guests in similar fashion. The room erupted in screams and chaos.

On the rooftop, the Major stepped forward into the yawning rush of the night and closed her eyes, embracing the wind. She plummeted like a falling knife down the side of the hotel tower, the windows flashing past her in a blur. Her eyes snapped open and she silently triggered an activation sequence. A wave of distortion seemed to envelop her, bleeding out color, turning her into a glassy apparition, a heat-haze mirage. The bodysuit's thermoptic camouflage was power-hungry and fragile, but it was enough to render her near-invisible.

"*Major!*" Aramaki cried into the comms again. He got no response.

The doors to the banquet suite crashed open and the six men entered, fanning out. Before the Hanka party and the West African retinue could react, the assassins opened fire without hesitation. They mowed down members of the African delegation and the Hanka Robotics team alike, seemingly at random. Still, when the shooting stopped, both Osmond and the president were still alive, albeit they were both crouched down and cowering in terror.

In an underground bunker, where light came primarily from the flickering devices all around, a man stood on the filthy and wet floor, watching the mayhem from the surveillance provided by the echo box. He needed no screen for this; the audio and video streams both fed into him directly via a vast network of cables plugged into a large apparatus on his neck. If this was uncomfortable, he showed no sign of it.

There was no one here with the man, no one to hide from in this secret place, but even so, he wore a hooded cloak that shadowed his features and concealed his form, making him look something like a medieval monk. He gave an order, seemingly to the air, in a voice that paused at odd moments, as though it was generated by a computer. "Initiate... the hack."

In the banquet room, the surviving guests whimpered, even more frightened now.

The red-clad geisha bot took no notice of any of them except Osmond. The synthetic leaned forward over him and, with a wet click, its delicate ceramic face split down the middle and snapped open. The bot's inner workings had been designed for function, not intimidation, so it was simply coincidence that it now looked like a cephalopod from the worst imaginings of a psychotic. Hungry cable tentacles writhed down out of its metal jaw and lunged into the bot's prey.

Osmond let out a pained gurgle and went limp as the geisha bot's cable heads locked into the open quik-ports on the back of his neck. He began to twitch like someone deep in REM sleep. His eyes became an opaque blue-white, like those of a day-old corpse. The neural jack was a penetrator device, a brute force cybernetic link capable of burning through any implanted firewalls and stripping a person's memories bare. The machine was hacking the contents of his mind.

Suddenly, gunshots smashed through a window, killing two of the gunmen and destroying one of the geisha bots. The humans spurted blood as they collapsed. The synthetic shut down in a messy, jerky heap, its body writhing and sparking, gushing thin streams of whitish liquid silicate.

The geisha holding Osmond, its face already distorted, now transformed further. Its legs twisted back against their joints in a way no human could ever have managed, and folded up around Osmond like a spider grasping its prey. The machine scuttled jerkily away across the carpeted floor, and then clambered *up* the wall. Hands becoming claws, the machine kept Osmond prisoner as it dragged itself and his insensate form up and out of reach, until the bot paused in a high corner of the ceiling.

More gunshots blasted through a different window, hitting and disabling another of the geisha bots. The four surviving gunmen fired back, roaring with inarticulate rage, their bullets shattering more glass and sending shards in a deadly rain to the street far below. The giant cyborg-spider was impervious, keeping its tight grip on Osmond as it continued to drain his data, even as yet other geisha bot was taken out.

Then an entire glass wall imploded. The Major smashed through it in a running leap, not slowed by the glass fragments that sliced into the room around and ahead of her, her pistol never pausing in its fire. The Major turned off her thermoptic camouflage as she entered the room, knowing that her sudden appearance would give her an added advantage by startling her adversaries. She used the momentum of her entrance to run up the wall, sprinting at a ninety-degree angle to the floor. In the moment it took the surviving gunmen to react, she acted on instinct, diving and firing, her semiautomatic pistol barking as she took down three more of the armed men with pinpoint shots to the head or the throat. An ordinary human operative would have never been able to move with such speed, but the Major was very far from *ordinary*. But as fast as she was, the Major could not avoid every bullet streaming in her direction and a round struck her left arm, forcing her to stifle a grunt of pain-feedback.

The two remaining intact geisha bots in black kimonos displayed more self-preservation than the human assassins by raising their arms in surrender.

The rest of the Section Nine team arrived in the street below beneath the massive purple sign identifying the Maciej. They raced under the exceptionally long entryway awning to the hotel's front door, passing a trio of splindly, non-fleshed synthetic servants.

The Major fired at the spider-like geisha bot in the red kimono. The shots found their mark. The stricken bot released Osmond. The man fell to the floor, dead. He hadn't been hit, but his brain was so traumatized by the bot's hack that it had shut down even the most basic impulses governing his lungs and heartbeat. The bioroid collapsed onto its back beside him, its legs crumpled over its back, fluids pooling around it as its wrecked systems began to shut down. It reached out to the Major with an arm.

The Major wasn't concerned—the bot was about to cease function at any moment. It couldn't hurt her. And then the bot spoke in a child's voice. "Help me. Please. Don't let me die."

The Major realized that the bioroid's gesture was not a threat, but an entreaty. This made so little sense that the Major almost didn't know how to respond. She stuck to her mission. "Who sent you?" she demanded.

The geisha spoke again, pleading. "Help me. Please."

"Answer me!" the Major insisted.

Then a different voice came through the geisha's speaker. It was male, both more and less mechanized-sounding that the geisha's speech had been. It was—although the Major had no way of recognizing it—the same voice that had instructed the geisha to hack Osmond. Now it said, "Collaborate with Hanka Robotics and be destroyed." The geisha opened the rest of its face, the cold metal petals folding outward to display the gold metal skull beneath.

The central cerebral processor module for Hanka's geisha model was mounted in the head, just behind what would have been the nasal cavity of a human being. A high-velocity bullet through the center of the face would crack it in two, immediately rendering the machine inert.

The Major was seldom unnerved, seldom moved to unnecessary action, but the geisha's pleas, followed by the terrorist threat, infuriated her. She emptied her pistol into the geisha's head until the unit was no longer operable. The mechanical face closed, returning to a semblance of normality as it ceased all function.

The Major stared at it, allowing herself to exhale, even as she wondered what the hell had just happened.

She heard hard breathing nearby. One of the gunmen was bleeding out, but still alive. He pulled a grenade from within his once-elegant suit jacket.

A booted foot ground down on his wrist and the gunman groaned weakly. Batou had arrived. The big Scandinavian calmly concentrated his weight onto his prisoner until he heard bones crack. The gunman gasped in agony.

Batou shook his head reprovingly. "Uh-uh." He ended the assassin's pain by putting a round through the man's skull. He scooped up the grenade, made sure the pin was securely in place, then went over to see how the Major was doing. "You okay?" He winced, inhaling softly as he got a better look at his colleague. "You're injured."

It took Batou's words to bring the Major out of her reverie. She raised her left arm to see a big red-rimmed wound that ran from her wrist to mid-forearm, exposing the robotic parts within, dripping the same kind of white liquid that had splattered out of the geisha bots she had destroyed. She looked down again at the one that had spoken to her, begged her…

Batou, better at reading the Major than anyone else in the Section, sensed that she felt some sort of kinship—totally unwarranted, in his view—with the wrecked machine on the floor. "You're not the same," he assured her.

The Major turned and headed for the door.

"Hey. *It's* just a robot!" Batou shouted after her.

The Major ignored Batou, heading outside as a squadron of local law enforcement, wearing vests that identified them as police, flooded into the room. She activated her thermoptic suit, becoming invisible once more. Some of the cops bumped into her, grunting in surprise at the unseen obstacle. She ignored them, too.

2

INNER UNIVERSE

There was no sense of transition for her, no moment of alteration from the dreaming world to her waking reality. Not anymore. It was just one of many tiny human things that she had lost, small details that no longer wove through her life.

At dawn, light filtered dimly in through the windows of the Major's apartment. Outside, a giant holographic woman was smiling over the harbor. The Major was fully conscious, though not yet dressed to go outside. She had on her sleep wear, a dark blue undershirt and shorts, as she sat up on her single-tatami bed, silently examining the damage she had sustained the night before. Instead of a mattress, the space beneath her body was a series of illuminated glass coils, a platform containing hidden sensors to scan her for signs of damage, and electromagnetically stimulate the nano-mech elements in her artificial bloodstream should any be found. The coils also generated a low-level power field capable of contact-charging her body's internal power supply while she was offline.

The bed could not repair the hole in her wrist, though. The bio-proxy skin had clotted around the edges of the ragged gouge in her flesh, but it hadn't knitted closed. The circuit matrix beneath was still visible. She would need to get one of the Section Nine mech-techs to take a look at that for her, but for now the limb seemed to be functioning adequately despite the surface damage.

Seeing the tech inside her surface flesh reminded the Major of the dying—no, de-activating—geisha bot that had said it didn't want to die. It had been fully mechanical, incapable of such sentiment. As a machine, it was also incapable of life in the first place, so it could not fear death. The begging must have been programmed by the terrorist who orchestrated the attack. And yet her own circuits did resemble those of the bot.

The Major knew there was no use in such thoughts. More important, there was no time for them. There was no day when her skills were not required by Section Nine. When she knew herself to be fully charged, she reached up to her neck to disengage the twin zeta-cables trailing from the ports there. The connectors came free with a metallic click and she let them drop away.

She stepped into what she thought of as the shower. It served the same function as a regular shower, though it only resembled one insofar as it was a stall. The Major hung suspended there while lights pulsed around her, emitting photosynthetic rays that cleaned detritus from her skin and refreshed the electrical impulses underneath.

When she was done, she dressed. Then she was startled by an organic noise that had no place in her sparsely furnished apartment: a meow.

The Major turned and saw, in a wall alcove, a grey-and-black striped tabby cat wearing a blue collar. The animal was up on her hind legs, reaching out with a front paw to bat at a bug. Then the cat momentarily broke into jagged video lines before vanishing completely.

She exhaled. It had been a glitch. The Major had been experiencing more of them lately. Nothing alarming, but she shouldn't have them. And why a cat, of all things? Maybe she'd subconsciously noticed a fragment of holo-advertising and it had lodged in her memory somehow. The image did seem familiar.

The Major opened a small package containing vials of yellow medication that kept the glitches at bay. She plugged one vial into the quik-port in her neck. When it was empty, she unplugged it, grabbed her jacket and left the apartment.

* * *

In the sky over the street, the gigantic hologram of a woman promoted something in Japanese. Garbled audio made her pitch indistinct. Besides, she was competing for airspace with a giant sologram billboard, which proclaimed in both text and a female voiceover, "Your skin deserves the best, and so do you. Try our hand cream."

More holo-ads filled the air around these, although none contained the leaping cat from the Major's glitch. The chill that made the other people on the street pull their coats tight didn't reach her as she threaded out of the habitat blocks and down through the narrow passages that led into the alley markets. A light rain was falling. A lot of people had umbrellas protecting their heads, but some either couldn't afford such luxuries or, like the Major, would rather get wet than not have their hands free.

She had a motorbike in the underground vehicle dock that could have taken her in across the loops and curves of the city's elevated highways, but something about the encounter in the Maciej the night before made her want to walk the distance to clear her mind. It wasn't an impulse she could have articulated, just a vague need to draw herself out of her own head, to move through the city and get lost for a little while in the ebb and flow of ordinary humanity.

The concrete canyons of the alleys extended away in every direction for kilometers, ribbons of asphalt barely wider than a subway carriage but all of them crammed with teeming swarms of humanity, along with quite a few synthetics. Her old MA-1 repro flight jacket simply helped her blend in; many people who weren't in the military liked to wear the clothing, in the hopes that it made them look tougher, less vulnerable.

Even at this early hour, with the sun just starting to climb over the peaks of the tallest habitat towers, the district was already busy. Vendors hawked all kinds of wares from every angle, some of them selling from inside makeshift bubble-tents or the gutted shells of cargo containers, fans of solar cells reaching up above them to provide power to lights or heater plates. Others worked out of their backpacks, sitting cross-legged in the middle of a blanket with a halo of goods spread out around them. The oldest and best-established pitches would actually have a veranda or maybe tables and chairs. The hot, greasy cooking smells of roasting meat and boiling noodles wafted up along the passages, mingling with the acrid tang of ozone and stale human sweat. The voices swirled around in a cacophony of languages, mostly Japanese, but enough others to make it sound like the whole world had gathered here to barter. The Major could credit neither her superior training nor unparalleled programming for her ability to ignore the clamor. Anyone who wanted to get anywhere on time in the city had learned to tune out distractions in order to arrive at their destination unhindered.

She joined the river of people moving westward, drifting with them at a walking pace. Many of the citizens passing by her were moving through worlds of their own, insulated from reality under digital hoods that fed them music or active video feeds, the enhanced media modules plugged directly into neural ports behind their ears. The more expensive modules provided not only sound and vision, but also a sensory component. It was possible to purchase high-end tech that would mask the real world with a virtual environment, so that if one preferred to walk through an art gallery or along a sunlit beach rather than down New Port City's choked streets, it was easy to do so.

The Major felt a prickle on her skin—intellectually, she knew that was not physically possible, because her dermal layer was precisely, uniformly controlled from her mech-core's central processor unit—but the psychosomatic response from her all-too-human brain made it feel real. She paid enough attention to the glowing yellow grids in the road to avoid being hit by traffic, but she also listened to her instinct, warily scanning the faces around her.

The Major reached the entrance to the National Security Force building that housed the Department of Defense Section Nine headquarters. There was nothing outside the building that indicated Section

Nine was within. In fact, it would be hard to find Section Nine on any organizational chart of the city's law enforcement hierarchy. Existing on a semi-covert level, the unit's grant of an exclusive counter-terrorist mandate meant that its operations often took place outside the public eye, with oversight only from the highest levels of government. Section Nine's corner of the public security arena went far beyond the remit of the more common crimes the police department dealt with, and they were situated above—figuratively and literally, in terms of floor placement—the special weapons and tactics divisions. In the articles of investiture that had allowed Section Nine to be created, there was vague language about "extraordinary threats" to the city's security and public welfare, and provisions for "extreme response" to "unseen dangers."

What that came down to in day-to-day operations was the use of a team of talented and diverse individuals—soldiers like the Major or Batou, former intelligence officers like Aramaki, or ex-cops like Togusa—to neutralize enhanced criminal and next-level terror threats.

It was a mission that made the Major feel like she was making a difference, and these days that was all that drove her onward.

Even on the primary floor entirely occupied by Section Nine, nothing about the place spoke to the unit's elite nature. A small staff of admin bioroids and technicians did most of the office chores while the core team concentrated on investigation and arrests. Off the grid from the city's other police units, they had no obvious precinct house for a potential enemy to target, and little footprint to leave them vulnerable to infiltration. If it wasn't for the ornamental shield on the wall, the entire floor could have been mistaken for some small-scale corporate data farm.

The Major glanced at the shield as she passed it. *Section Nine—Cyber Terror Response Division.* Quite what the ministry thought of their near-clandestine unit wasn't something that the Major or her team spent much time dwelling on. There was always another operation coming down the line, always another threat on the horizon.

The others were already in the building and followed the Major into the conference room. It was expansive and mostly bare. Couches ringed the walls, but the space was otherwise unfurnished. The evidence the team studied was mainly in the form of three-dimensional holograms; it would have been foolish to clutter up the central viewing area with a table and chairs.

As the team filed in, the Major sensed a familiar crackle of tension in the air—the same cocktail of anticipation and unspent energy she had experienced a hundred times before, on missions and out on the battlefield. Each member of the unit had been recruited because of a skill set that fitted Section

Nine's remit, each one of them in the top percentile of their capabilities. Of course, that also meant that their personalities didn't quite always mesh, but in the field that never seemed to be a problem. Whatever their quirks or differences were outside of operations, all of them were professional enough to put them aside when the guns came out.

Batou, big and bearded, self-consciously ran a hand through his bleached hair and managed a wan smile at the Major. He looked troubled, but then he almost always did. Batou was her strong right arm out in the world, thanks to a firm partnership between them that had formed out of an unconscious acceptance that they worked well together. Before Section Nine, Batou had been a member of the Swedish Army's Special Operations Group, and he took orders without question.

Togusa was the newest member of the team. The guy was pure police through and through. He retained the formality of his old detective unit, wearing a suit and tie on the job even in Section Nine. He was also a rarity in the city, a near-untouched natural human with no more than the most basic enhancement implants in his body—and still he had been putting away crooks bristling with cyber-tech at a rate that had earned him a bunch of commendations. The Major had warmed to the guy from the start; Togusa was honest and showed himself willing to get right into the thick of things.

Ladriya was the tough Anglo-Indian who handled their on-site tech. She was also the only woman on the team besides Major. When Ladriya talked, she sounded as though she came from south or east London, though her family was originally from somewhere in southeast Asia. To hear Ladriya tell it, her folks hadn't been thrilled that instead of taking a job close to home, she'd wound up all the way in New Port City, doing work she could never discuss in her weekly video chats with Mum and Dad. The Major was grateful for Ladriya's wanderlust. The woman's technical skills were part of what kept the team on the bleeding edge, and like most of Section Nine, she was more interested in results than in salutes and protocol. Today, Ladriya sported a sonic piece on her right ear for work and a gold ornament on her left as an assertion of personality.

Ladriya was carefully ignoring Borma, whose machine-optic eye implants raked over the room. If there had ever been something between those two, it had never followed them to the job. What the Major knew about Ladriya's professional past was the kind of deliberately hazy narrative that belonged to someone from the intelligence community. Borma and his skill with explosives suggested a former career as a demolitions specialist.

Saito, the group's primary sniper, glanced in her direction, his unblinking hawk-eye implant fixing her for a brief instant. He came from a mercenary background, from years working as a private military contractor, and he was another of Aramaki's personal recruits. She wondered what had swayed Saito away from a lucrative profession as a shooter-for-hire and into a new role with Section Nine. As always, the chief played his cards close to his chest on that matter, and Saito was in no hurry to open up about it.

Ishikawa, the last member of the team, was Section Nine's resident information warfare specialist. He had his father's surname, his mother's Afro-Caribbean good looks, and almost the same London accent as Ladriya. Ishikawa also looked very young, just out of his teens, despite his scruffy beard. Something seemed off about him this morning, and it wasn't just his usual hangover.

"So, what do we have on Osmond?" the Major asked.

Ladriya knew that the immediate information was required. She was sorry she didn't have more to give. "So far, very little." She turned on the holo-floor in the middle of the room, which projected three-dimensional images of the late Dr. Osmond. Everyone took a seat to view the data. "He was the head of Hanka's robotics division. Human, but of course cyber-enhanced."

They all knew a man in that position would have had the most highly developed cyber-protection in existence implanted in his neural system. Batou voiced what everyone was thinking. "So, how did they hack him?"

The hologram now displayed the fatal attack on Osmond in the banquet hall. The Major indicated the action being played back in the hologram. "Somehow this geisha bot got past his encryption."

It was never wise to ignore the Major, but Togusa couldn't help it. He was distracted by a change in Ishikawa. The man had had some sort of new cyber-enhancement done, made more provocative because Togusa couldn't readily decipher what it was. "Something's different."

Ishikawa sighed softly.

Togusa refused to be put off. "What'd you get?"

"Why you always think he's out there enhancin'?" Ladriya teased. Ishikawa had a few low-level neural enhancements and a couple of simple bio-modifications, but it was an open secret that he wanted more than that. These days, it was the equivalent of what getting a new piercing or a tattoo had been, back when those had been considered slightly daring.

"Because he is," Togusa replied, defending his original question.

Ishikawa removed all doubt by pulling up his shirt and displaying the crimson line of a fresh surgical scar across his belly. "Cyber-mech liver," he explained. This was a combination of computerized and robotic components. "Been savin' up for a while." He grinned. "Now it's last call every night."

Togusa was appalled. "You got enhanced so you can drink more?"

Ishikawa grinned wickedly, clicked his tongue and winked.

Ladriya gave a snort of laughter at Togusa's reaction. "Embrace the enhancements, Togusa. Me and the Major? We wouldn't be here without it." True enough. Almost everyone on the team had been wounded in action at some point and had required cyber enhancements to save their lives. And everyone knew the Major was nothing *but* cyber enhancements, except for her brain.

Togusa hoped the Major didn't take offense, but he was proud of the fact that all of his skills were honed by practice and experience, not technology. "I'm all human... and happy, thanks."

The Major did not respond to his words. Instead, she remained focused on the mission. "Any more information on the ceased geisha bot?"

The holographic display now showed the red-clad bot that had pleaded with the Major; lists of printed information scrolled alongside the image.

"Hanka's running scans," Togusa said. "Dr. Dahlin will have the report ready by—"

He broke off abruptly as the hologram of the geisha bot vanished, replaced by the Section Nine S9 logo as Chief Aramaki entered the conference room.

3

INTERFACED

Everyone rose swiftly and stood at attention on Aramaki's arrival. The chief did not bother with verbal greetings. Unlike most men commanding military units, Section Nine's top officer did not shave or crop his hair. Instead, he wore it in a style that was wide on either side at the top and tapered in more closely to frame his lined and firm features, giving him the look of an old but still fierce lion that was for some reason inside an office building instead of out prowling the veldt. He perpetually wore the kind of stern expression that was better suited to some hard-ass schoolteacher or an unforgiving mob boss.

At the chief's nod, everyone in the team sat down on the couches again. "I have been speaking with the prime minister," Aramaki informed his subordinates. "He wants a full report. Togusa." Aramaki indicated that the man should speak.

Togusa obediently activated a hidden control, and the room dimmed as a crimson-hued hologram display rose up out of the floor and swiftly sketched in a series of holograms showing three different people that the Major had never seen before. Aramaki sat now as well, concentrating, as Togusa summed up what they'd uncovered so far. "Following last night's attack, three more Hanka scientists were murdered at the company's central laboratory." There had been several other recent Hanka deaths, but those had, until now, been chalked up to ill fortune with petty criminals and coincidence. No more—even without the attack in the banquet room, this proved a pattern.

"The first two were shot," Togusa continued, inhaling softly as he indicated two of the holograms, "and the third was beaten to death by his own service robot." He moved to indicate the third hologram, which displayed a dead scientist slumped over a desk that had fist-sized holes pounded into it. "All showed signs of cerebral hacking." Togusa manipulated the hologram so that it now focused on the dead man's quik-port.

"The same as the geisha did to Osmond," Togusa added, even though his colleagues were well aware of this. "And all were senior figures in Hanka. Just like Osmond. A message was left at each of the crime scenes by someone identifying himself..."

Togusa brought up a new hologram. It was fuzzy and incomplete, but part of a face was clear, a young

Caucasian man peering out from under a hood. Togusa finished, "...as Kuze."

The same voice and the same warning the Major had heard in the banquet room now came from the hologram. "Collaborate with Hanka Robotics and be destroyed. Collaborate with Hanka Robotics and be destroyed."

Section Nine had considered the possibility that the murders were anti-tech bio-purity militants or counter-capitalists targeting Hanka as part of their agenda, but those theories appeared increasingly unlikely. The attacks seemed designed to demonstrate that enhanced minds could be hacked, without consent, without control.

Batou felt his skin crawl a little, but he ignored it. It was the secret fear of everyone with a neural interface: no matter how good your firewall, there was a chance you could fall prey to a mind-hack. He made a mental note to check his interface barrier software for an update when the briefing was over, just to be on the safe side.

Aramaki spoke decisively. "Togusa. You and Ladriya go speak to Mr. Cutter, the CEO of Hanka. Major and Batou, get Dahlin's report. Find out what she recovered from the geisha."

Batou stood and bowed to his commander. "Aramaki."

"Major!" Aramaki said, before the Major could follow. The chief stood, indicating she should follow him into his adjoining office as the rest of the agents exited the conference room by the opposite door.

Two female attendants shut the double doors behind the Major, then stood silently to either side. The Major had never heard either of them speak in the entire year she'd been with the Section. So far as she knew, both women were entirely human, but they'd had some sort of neural enhancement that allowed them to stand unmoving for hours.

The chief's office brought together tradition and technology. There was a bonsai tree on a side table, which Aramaki had painstakingly cultivated himself. The furniture was a combination of dark carved wood and leather. One of the walls was green marble shot through with white. The desktop was made of the same marble, with a single plain teacup sitting on its surface. The wall behind the desk was alight with shimmering green circuitry. The Major waited, standing, as Aramaki sat down behind his desk, facing away from her and staring at the circuitry, as though it might give him insight into her rebellious actions.

Aramaki smacked his lips, then spoke. "I told you not to jump."

"I had to, or more would have died," the Major countered.

Aramaki's tone made it clear he did not accept her explanation for the previous night's exploits. "You are a member of my team, and my responsibility."

The Major wanted to make it clear that she

understood her own responsibility when it came to the terrorist Kuze. "I will find him, and I will kill him. It's what I am built for, isn't it?"

Aramaki at last turned in his chair to face the Major, then held her gaze as he spoke with uncharacteristic softness. "You are more than just a weapon. You have a soul… a ghost." He paused for a moment, thinking how best to help the single-minded woman before him connect with her own humanity, no matter how violent her work. "When we see our uniqueness as a virtue, only then do we find peace."

The Major bowed her head to him, in gratitude as well as formal farewell. It was more than kind of Aramaki to take time to speak to her so personally. She only wished she knew how to take his advice.

The streets were even busier, if that was possible, than they had been in the morning. The Major and Batou, both clad in jeans and jackets to blend in, adroitly made their way on foot through the pedestrians and peddlers heading in all directions. Many of the people were too distracted by their own tech to watch where they were going.

Above, one floating billboard for Locus Slocus depicted a doctor giving a flower to a child, "Safely reconfiguring your child's genetic structure. Families: built better."

Given all of the drama, real and fictional, based on

men's concerns about making sure their genes were passed down through successive generations, Batou wondered how that particular technology would fare with the public, but he had more important matters to discuss with the Major, starting with her strange reaction to the deactivated geisha bot. "What was going on with you at the hotel last night?"

"Nothing," the Major declared, not looking at him. "I'm fine."

A pair of beat cops hurried past, their uniforms flashing the word POLICE.

"You sure?" Batou pressed.

Before the Major could respond, a male street hustler emerged from the crowd, targeting the Major with his spiel. He wore a turquoise snakeskin jacket over a white t-shirt, and the entire left side of his face was covered in mech. He smelled as if he'd spent the last week without showering while he sampled his own product, which was likely the case. "Hey, sweetheart," the hustler began, zeroing in on the Major.

"Move," Batou said. He tried to get between the punk and the Major, but the idiot ignored him.

"You want an upgrade?" the hustler crooned.

Batou glared. Some street dealer offering illegal cyber-enhancement to the Major, of all people, might be comical if it wasn't so annoying. "Move," Batou repeated.

"I have anything you want," the hustler promised.

Batou lost it. "Back off!" He gave the man a

hard shove, sending him tumbling backwards. The dealer's squawk of pain was drowned out by a loud male Japanese-speaking hologram and the giggles of two nearby girls, who were apparently amused by the altercation.

And still the Major didn't react. She was hard to read at the best of times, but Batou thought she seemed unusually remote today.

They reached a marketplace full of food vendors. The smells and sounds were as varied as the languages. Sweet, sour, savory, salty—whatever anyone might want to eat, it was all here for the best prices in the city, as the vendors were quick to shout from their stalls.

Batou spotted a butcher he knew and called out, "Hey, Ming!"

"Hey, Batou!" the butcher called back, coming out of his stall. "I got your bones." He handed over a bag filled with animal bones and scraps of meat, whatever leftovers he couldn't sell for human consumption.

"Thanks, man."

Ming gave him a nod that said Batou was entirely welcome. It certainly beat having the offal sitting in the booth's garbage cans, attracting rats and stinking up the place until the weekly trash pick-up. Ming added, "See you soon."

Batou saw the Major's cocked eyebrow. He was pleased to see something had piqued her curiosity, even if it was something as mundane as the contents of the bag. "For the dogs," he explained.

Batou turned down a dark, damp alley. The Major followed. "For someone who doesn't like people, how come you care about dogs so much?" she said.

Batou shrugged, his bleached hair the one bright focal point in the alley's dimness. "Don't know. I just like strays, and they like me."

"They like you 'cause you feed them," the Major pointed out.

They passed a delivery man pounding for entry on a dingy metal door, despite the holographic sign proclaiming, CLOSED 11AM–4PM.

Batou hoped the noise wouldn't scare off the dogs. "You got no heart," he teased the Major. He didn't mean it, and she knew that, but he did think there was more to stray dogs than simple hunger.

Sure enough, four dogs came out of the shadows, tails wagging. "Hey, girls!" Batou was happy to see them, and so far as he could tell, they were happy to see him. Two were large and black, their breeds unknown, and one was some kind of German Shepherd mix. Batou whistled and began feeding them before a smaller dog—a basset hound—trotted up to him. Batou made sure the little guy got his fair share. "Hey, Gabriel," he said to the canine. "Meet Major." Then he looked up. "Major, Gabriel."

Gabriel wagged his tail and while the Major said nothing, she smiled down at the dog.

* * *

Later, the rain came down harder. Batou and the Major were in his car on one of the many downtown highways, where a holo billboard above touted, "With Digital Pharmacies, you can erase painful memories." The vehicle was a modified Lotus that would have been at home on any racetrack in Europe. It was sleek, black with silver accents, low to the ground, with a roof that slanted downward over the front seat. Batou told everyone he'd bought the car for its speed and precise handling, but everyone knew as well as he did that its appearance had been a powerful factor in his purchase decision.

The Major had been silent since the alley. Batou thought she might talk about the investigation, or why she had been so troubled, but when she finally spoke, she said, "We used to have a dog."

Batou looked over at her. "Seriously?" He chuckled, surprised. "I had you down as more of a cat person."

Now the Major chuckled as well.

"You don't talk about that stuff, huh?" Batou observed.

The Major frowned slightly, not sure what he meant. "What?"

"Your past." He hoped the question wouldn't cause her to shut him out again.

Her answer was honest. "Well, I don't remember much. Just fragments. Bits and pieces."

"What about family?" Batou asked.

The Major still couldn't even find a sense of genuine sorrow, only regret that she could access neither the memories nor the feelings they ought to have caused. "My parents," she told Batou, "they died bringing us to this country." She remembered there had been a dissident crackdown in their homeland, that the authorities had been after her father, that it seemed too dangerous to stay. But she couldn't remember their home clearly, or exactly what her father had done that put him at so much risk that they had to leave. She could not even remember whether she had seen her parents go into the water when the boat sank, or if they'd been somewhere else on the deck. She barely even remembered what they looked like. Ouelet had said that the memories would gradually come back, that she was still suffering psychologically from what had happened and that her mind was distancing itself from the events until she could emotionally deal with the trauma. The Major hoped that was true. She clearly remembered everything since waking up in the Hanka operating room well enough, but of course she had cybernetic memory upgrades to help with that. "Our boat sank in the harbor. I almost drowned. And it feels like..." The Major found that she wanted Batou to understand how things were for her, why she wasn't better at being a friend to him, to anyone. "There's always this thick fog over my memory and I can't see through it."

"You're lucky," Batou replied. "Every single day I get screwed by my memories." That was putting it mildly. Batou inhaled. He wished he could forget what had happened, what had been done to him and, worst of all, what he had done. He thought it was a miracle he hadn't lost his mind. "It's better to be pure." He exhaled. "Like you."

The Major smiled in response and chuckled again, mostly at the suggestion that she was pure. She couldn't recall her life before Section Nine, but she doubted what she'd done since joining the task force fit anyone's definition of "pure," even Batou's.

She looked out the window, and for a moment saw something very strange. There, in the middle of the intersection, with vehicles driving all around it, was a small pagoda made of brown wood. She stared at it. And then it flashed, de-resolved and vanished. Just like the cat in her apartment this morning. Another glitch.

They made good time along the expressway and into the corporate sector, before Batou brought his car into a parking bay in the shadow of a huge glass office tower. The Major snapped off her seatbelt and climbed out, taking a breath of cool air.

Up here, in the sector of the city where wealth flowed freely, it was a world away from the habitat levels choked with people. Around them, elegantly-manicured lawns and abstract pieces of sculpture dotted a vast plaza of clean lines and steel arches. The headquarters of the big mega-corps rose out of the white stone and reached high into the sky, each of them like glassy fortresses emblazoned with company logos.

The Hanka Robotics tower was a place the Major was as familiar with as her own apartment. The building bore the company logo and had its own entrance plaza, decorated with early robotic prototypes. One silver replica of an antique robot loomed almost two stories high. Hanka was also famous for its weapons systems, and replicas of these were on display as well, including a small multi-legged tank that looked like a giant artificial spider. A female voice wafted over the plaza's public address system: "Welcome to Hanka Robotics."

It felt odd to be here on public security business instead of for more personal reasons, but the Major pushed that thought away and followed Batou through the entry grid. The voice over the PA continued: "All visitors must display appropriate credentials at all times."

In Ouelet's operating room, the Major sat while delicate-looking instruments, attached to a semi-circular arc, repaired the robotics within her injured left arm. The skin had been removed from her hand, leaving the metal fingers bare for easier access. The epidermis would be replaced when the work was completed. Her quik-port was attached to Ouelet's small, flat computer so that the doctor could read the Major's data, which scrolled down in cascading lines of gold text through the air, like rain on a windowpane.

"Open and close, please," Ouelet directed.

The Major obediently flexed her skinless left hand.

"You have damaged internal systems," Ouelet noted. With only minor surgery going on, the doctor still wore sterile slippers, but the red scrubs were gone. Instead, the doctor was clad in a translucent aqua lab coat over pale hospital garb.

The look suited Genevieve's gentle nature, the Major thought. She grinned. "Maybe next time you can design me better."

Ouelet replied with a soft chuckle as she smiled back. There was genuine warmth in her expression, and in her words as she asked, "How are you?"

"I'm fine," the Major replied. It was true—it was annoying that the circuitry in her hand had been impacted by the bullet, but her wrist didn't hurt. Nothing hurt. "I can't feel anything."

"No," Ouelet persisted, "*you*. In there." The doctor never let an opportunity pass to remind the Major that she still possessed a human brain and, therefore, according to Ouelet, a human soul.

"I've been having glitches." The Major's confession

was reluctant. "But they'll pass."

Ouelet registered concern. "Have you been taking your medication?"

"Yeah. But these ones are still cycling." Remembering both the cat and the pagoda, the Major added, "I had two this morning."

"Sound or image?"

"Both."

Ouelet picked up the portable computer terminal that was still plugged into the Major. A waterfall of complex data tumbled down the screen, the dense lines of neural patterning code that were Mira Killian's higher brain functions. The doctor peered at the strings of information and nodded, indicating that the glitches were revealed in what she was reading. "I see it. Have you made any unencrypted downloads?"

The Major frowned slightly. "No." Taking action when circumstances demanded, as she had in the banquet room, was one thing. Risky behavior for its own sake was something else entirely. Some people loved the thrill and the danger, but the Major would sooner drink from a sewer line than make an unencrypted download; the sewage wouldn't do much harm to her synthetic organs, whereas the download could leave her vulnerable to hacks or even destroy her internal network. And Genevieve Ouelet, of all people, knew this. "Just delete them for me."

Ouelet nodded. "Consent?" The question was a legal formality. Any cyber-enhancement user had to give their official consent to any manipulation of their data, including deletion of glitches.

The Major observed the formality in turn. "My name is Major Mira Killian, and I give my consent to delete this data."

With a few practiced finger strokes, Ouelet deleted the glitches and put down the terminal. "It's done." Seeing that the Major still looked troubled, she added, "No big deal." She unplugged the cables from the Major's quik-port.

But the Major wanted more information about the glitches. "What are they?"

Ouelet inhaled, contemplating how to phrase her answer. She kept her voice light. "Sensory echoes from your mind. Shadows. Can't be sure."

The Major wasn't satisfied. "Well, how do you know what's a glitch and what's me?" With so few memories from before she had been installed in the synthetic shell, she couldn't be sure herself.

"The glitches have a different texture... to the rest of your code." Ouelet swallowed uneasily, then smiled again. "I can see everything. All of your thoughts, your... decisions."

Even when it was Genevieve scanning the data, the Major was perturbed by this absolute invasion of her thoughts. "I guess privacy is just for humans."

"You *are* human." There was an urgency in Ouelet's voice now. She wanted the Major to believe as she believed. "People *see* you as human."

The Major wondered how it was that Ouelet, even with data access to every thought and experience, still didn't understand what it was like. "Everyone around me seems to fit. They seem connected to something. Something I am... not." She paused, trying to find exactly what she wanted to say. "It's like I have no past."

"Of course you have a past." Ouelet's voice was reassuring, though she was turned to look at something else in the room. "And with time, you'll feel more and more connected to it, and to them."

Ouelet returned her attention to the Major's arm. The equipment had finished making repairs and new unmarked skin covered the area, as though no injury had ever occurred.

"Open and close, please."

The Major opened and closed her fist again. The fingers and wrist moved exactly as they should and the skin showed no signs of strain.

Ouelet smiled. "Ah." She affectionately ran her hand over the healed forearm and returned to what was really bothering the Major. "We cling to memories as if they define us, but they really don't." Ouelet paused and put her hand on the Major's shoulder, her gesture and words both offering comfort. "What we *do* is what defines us."

Batou had waited with as much patience as he could

muster outside Ouelet's office. He'd called Ishikawa to send in some analytics techs to make sure he hadn't missed something at the crime scene, but he was glad he was to be on the move again when the Major finally emerged.

As the two of them headed down yet another hallway in the endless maze that was Hanka Robotics, this one leading to the Forensics Department, a female voice announced, "You are entering a Hanka secure area. Authorized personnel only. Please disable communications enhancements."

The Major and Batou disabled their internal comms and entered the forensics lab. The cybernetic morgue was a cross between a dystopian hospital and the inside of a machine shop. Unlike a regular morgue for humans, the data forensics lab was kept at uniformly blood-warm temperature—reportedly the optimal atmosphere for preserving magnetic bubble memory substrates, or something like that. Batou didn't care about the reason, he just knew that being in here made him uncomfortable.

As he trailed after the Major into the main lab, he pulled at his collar and looked around. The geisha bot that had hacked its way into Paul Osmond's grey matter was lying on a steel operating table, its mechanical innards open to the waist. Its faceplates were peeled back in their flower-like, open configuration, showing the gold-hued cyber skull beneath. The eye sockets were empty. Red, blue and black cables dangled out of the mouth like dead tentacles.

Bent over the slab in the center of the blue-tiled room was Dr. Sonia Dahlin. She had her light brown hair cut fashionably short and slicked back from her forehead, and her makeup was well applied to maximize her appeal in a non-showy way, but her manner was matter-of-fact to the point of brusqueness.

The lab's window had an unexciting view of a row of unfinished bots, their female gender made evident by their bare metal breasts. A male bot in shapeless orange clothing stood inactive in the doorway.

The techno-pathologist had her hands deep inside the geisha bot's torso. Dahlin didn't look up, but her tone made it clear she didn't appreciate having visitors. "I'm busy."

Batou found the pathologist's obvious desire for solitude just too tempting. "Dr. *Daaahlin*!" he drawled, as if he was overjoyed to be in her presence, and she likewise couldn't wait to see him. He knew how irritated she'd be by his pretend familiarity. "Are you finished yet?" He also knew the insinuation that she worked too slowly would irritate her even more.

Dahlin still didn't look up, but her tone suggested she wouldn't mind if it was Batou on her slab instead of the bot. "If you hadn't riddled the geisha with bullets, this would be much easier."

Now Batou feigned hurt. "I didn't shoot her."

The Major kept it simple. "I did."

Dahlin finally favored them both with a weary

glance. She knew Section Nine needed results right away, but forensic scans and analysis of the sheer amount of data would take a while She sighed. "This is gonna take days. I need to run hundreds of potential simulations."

"We don't have the time," said the Major, confirming Dahlin's timeframe fears.

Dahlin tried to explain the complexity of the problem. "She was a Hanka companion bot. But she was reprogrammed for cerebral hacking."

As the two women talked, Batou wandered over to another slab and, curious, pulled back the sheet. One of the dead gunmen from the banquet room massacre lay there, as lifeless as the geisha bot. The gunman's torso and head were human, but his arms were robotic and there were wires protruding from his eye sockets.

"What was on her drives?" the Major asked.

"Nothing," Dahlin replied. "The data was destroyed as it was transmitted. No sign what she was after." Whatever had been stolen from Osmond's brain was now in the hands of the terrorist who had engineered the hack. He had made sure nothing was left behind that could lead back to him or even suggest what he ultimately wanted. "The hardware was vandalized. They ripped her up."

The Major briefly contemplated their options. She leaned in over the dead machine's broken shell. "Then I have to do a Deep Dive." This was the term for the complex process whereby one cyber-consciousness fully meshed with another for investigative purposes.

Dahlin, who as a scientist should have been on board with this, objected. "You can't encrypt during a Deep Dive."

"I know." The irony of her earlier exchange with Ouelet about not downloading unencrypted data was not lost on the Major; a Deep Dive into a terrorist-corrupted bot would be infinitely more hazardous. But the investigation was in danger of stalling, and she didn't want to wait for another Hanka Robotics executive to be murdered. What if the next body to drop was Genevieve Ouelet? She would never be able to forgive herself.

Dahlin took a soft, annoyed breath, pushed herself away from the slab, then rattled off the ugly possibilities. "They could have left traps in her. Mag pulses. Viruses."

As Dahlin sat down behind a control console, Batou for once took the pathologist's side. "Mm, she's right." The Major gave him a look but Batou was not deterred. "You'll be exposing your mind to whoever hacked her. You'll be wide open."

He wasn't saying anything that all of them didn't already know. "I have to get inside her memory," the Major replied. The geisha had had a functioning memory right up to the moment bullets had obliterated her cranial hardware. The Major removed her pistol, then began taking off her jacket. "It's the fastest way to find Kuze."

Dahlin put a cigarette to her lips, clicked a square lighter to get a flame and took a pull, trailing thin vapor. Never known for her humanitarian concern, she was still opposed to letting the Major take the risk. "It's too dangerous. And highly irresponsible."

The Major didn't offer any further verbal argument. Instead, she sat on the empty slab next to the one holding the geisha.

Batou grabbed a cable and held it out to the Major. He was so worried that she could hear it in the way he breathed, but ultimately, he was always on her side. "Are you sure?" he asked.

The Major nodded. "You see any bad code headed my way, pull me out." She knew Batou would stop the Deep Dive at the first sign of trouble.

He sighed, but guided a zeta-cable into the Major's lower neck ports. He then ran the cable through an echo box splitter that routed the data to the pathologist's command terminal. As the other woman connected the synthetic to the rig, the Major lay back, and regarded Batou's grim expression.

She flashed a near-smile at him and joked, "How come *you're* the one sweating?"

Batou didn't smile back. Instead, he sighed again and turned to Dahlin, resigned. "Run it."

Dahlin emitted her own sigh, expressing skepticism, and extinguished her cigarette into a glass of water full of floating butts. Then she raised a detachable section of her cyber-enhanced face, so that her eyes and temple appeared to be in front of her forehead, revealing the quik-ports installed in her eye sockets. She inserted a virtual-reality monitoring device into the quik-ports, so that she could maintain contact with the Major through the Dive.

Then Dahlin flicked a switch on the console and spoke formally into a data recorder pick-up, reciting the mandated legal jargon. "Cyber-mind connection to the Major now active and unencrypted. Consent required for data download."

The Major, lying on the slab with her eyes closed, gave the mandated response. "My name is Major Mira Killian, and I give my consent."

Dahlin input a command to execute the program and, in the real world, the Major twitched on the slab.

A split second later, the Major felt the zeta-cable in her neck go hot. The cable sparkled with amber data that bore her consciousness into the geisha bot, and the Dive began with a swooping, vertiginous sensation. She had done this before, but every time was different, each Dive a new shock to the system. She felt herself fall down through the slab, and then plummet down to the bottom of the sea. It was like her memories of drowning, except that instead of being pulled to safety, here she kept descending through the deep, inky waters, never to be found. And then she fell further, through the geisha bot's broken face.

In the void between the ticks of the clock, the

Major's consciousness was projected into the non-space of the geisha's synthetic mind. She saw a light. Streamers of broken, faltering code shot past her, falling meteorites of dying data that burned out as they became nothingness.

It was a continuous stream of motion-recall, and as she fell into it, suddenly she was seeing the recent past through the dead machine's eyes. Beyond the flickering code was a three-dimensional space. The voice of a companion bot spoke, too close to come from anywhere but her own throat, and the Major understood that she was doing the talking, even though the ultra-feminine Japanese-accented voice was nothing like her own. "*Konnichiwa*," said the companion bot, uttering the Japanese word for "hello." She expressed formal gratitude in both English and Japanese. "Thank you. *Arigatou gozaimasu...*"

The Major could see that she was in a contemporary nightclub. The hostesses, bartenders, gangster customers and companion bots crowding the place were all frozen in time, though a neon sign on the wall flickered. It read, "Sound Business." The name suggested the owners were fond of puns, as it proclaimed both that the establishment was run prudently, and that the music pulsing from the club's many speakers was one of its chief attractions.

The still images crumbled, data bytes dissolving like columns of ash, then resolved further along, showing the same people in new poses. The Major made her way through the unmoving patrons and waitresses, searching for the geisha bot. There were plenty of real women and companion bots here, but none were the one she sought. It unsettled the Major that she could hear running conversations around her, even though the people were statue-still. They also looked ghostly, as if they had all died yet remained upright.

"Thank you," the companion bot repeated. Her words echoed slightly. "*Arigatou gozaimasu.*" This was followed by a burst of laughter from some of the customers, and rapid comments in Japanese.

The Major, the only moving figure in the room, found the red-robed geisha near the back of the club. She was surprised to find that this version looked more like a real woman in a geisha mask than a bot with a painted faceplate. Before the Major could begin to examine the geisha, the images in the nightclub moved, as though someone was shifting a series of life-sized photos or sculptures.

Suddenly, a burly thug grabbed the geisha, which uttered a frightened protest, but in a low voice. Her ingrained fear of disrupting the club's patrons was greater than her fear of assault.

The thug ignored the geisha entirely and said, "Yes," in Japanese.

The images crumbled again, and now the burly man was dragging the geisha through a back door.

The Major followed. She had lost sight of both the geisha and her abductor, but the geisha's agonized shriek sent the Major running in the direction of the sound. She could also hear the thug's cruel laughter and taunts as she went through the back door and down a long hallway. It was dark and grimy and smelled of chemicals.

The Major found herself in a large basement work room. She was presented with another frozen tableau, this one of a man in a dark cloak with the hood pulled up over his head. He was performing a hack on a supine geisha bot clad in white. This image, unlike the rest, did not crumble and give way. Even without seeing his face, the Major knew the cloaked figure was Kuze—and, unlike the rest of the individuals she'd seen so far in the Deep Dive, he was not motionless. Kuze turned and thrust out his arm like a magician casting a spell—

And the Major was flung back into darkness. She could just make out movement around her, and then she was surrounded by scores of black, decaying robots that were intent on tearing off the bioroid flesh from her synthetic bones. The machines crowded in, closer and closer...

In the forensics lab, Batou saw the Major trembling violently on the slab. Her shoulders shook and her back arched.

Batou could see she was in trouble. "Disconnect," he ordered Dahlin. "Get her out."

The Major grunted and twitched, imprisoned in the Dive's code. "Get her out!" Batou shouted this time.

"I'm trying!" Dahlin snapped back. "But she's being hacked."

This only made the situation worse, as far as Batou was concerned. "*Get her out now!*"

In the Deep Dive, the Major yelled in desperation as the swarm of predatory, ruined robots closed in around her.

In the forensics lab, the Major convulsed.

Dahlin frantically typed commands into her instruments. Her hands weren't free, so she called to Batou, "Now!"

Batou grabbed the cable and, with a grunt of effort, yanked it out of the Major's quik-port, releasing her from the Deep Dive.

The zeta-cable was supposed to be removed from the quik-ports slowly and carefully, so when it was suddenly torn away, the Major sat bolt upright. Batou put his hands firmly on her shoulders so that she wouldn't fall. Her eyes were wide and unfocused in terror. She shuddered and gasped, trying to get her bearings.

Batou was trying to catch his own breath. What had happened to the Major in there? Was she still herself? Did she know where she was now? Was there anything he could do to help her? He expressed all of this with, "Are you okay?"

The Major managed to control her breathing

enough to speak. "I know where he is."

4

SOUND BUSINESS

Downtown New Port City was the city's vampire district, a place that lay near-dead and dormant during daylight hours, but came to neon-fueled life at night as the reckless or the dangerous congregated in its bars, nightclubs and drinking pits. These establishments nestled beneath the skyscrapers, rather the way cockroaches congregated under blocks of cement.

Just off the main drag, an alley led to a black-framed door retrofitted with atmosphere processors, where a garish illuminated sign gave the promise of illicit thrills within. The Sound Business club looked exactly as it had in the memories of the dead geisha synthetic. Batou, protected against the night air by a long brown coat that—not coincidentally—could conceal all manner of items, made his way over to where the Major and Ladriya were waiting for him. A collection of discs and an empty metal frame were propped up against the alley wall, looking like three-dimensional punctuations in the copious graffiti all around. Ladriya, in a padded jacket with a bright blue and green pattern, looked up, acknowledging Batou's arrival.

The Major had changed into a red jumpsuit with diagonal zippers to sell the fiction that she was just some well-off dilettante from the corporate zone, slumming it down here for kicks.

"I know this place," Batou said, keeping his voice soft. "They run black-market mech. You tooled up?"

Ladriya indicated her well-armed backpack. "Yep."

The Major nodded, mentally reconstructing what she had gleaned of the club's layout from her Deep Dive into the synthetic's mind. "Target's the basement," she instructed the others. "I'll lead. Switching to mind-comms." Pure humans did not have the ability to process mental information as data. The Major had insisted that using spoken word over the mind-comms enabled her to communicate with her team more quickly. She pulled a medication vial out of her quik-port, then looked back at Batou. "Hope you've been practicing." He was a great practical fighter, but he sometimes forgot not to speak aloud when the comms were in use.

"That's unfair!" Batou called after the Major as she headed out of the alley. Then he remembered to turn on his comm. "It just takes me a moment to—"

he realized he was still speaking out loud and finally switched to the mind-comm, "—*get the hang of it*."

On the far side of the street from the nightclub, a threadbare noodle bar wreathed in steam was doing slow business, with only a couple of diners sitting on the benches with their faces in bowls of ramen. One of them was Togusa, who paused to tap his own implant and then continued to eat.

Above, a billboard advertised "sexy lipstick" in Cantonese, and all around, people on the street were chattering and laughing. The Major headed into Sound Business. The club's front door led straight to a staircase that funneled guests to the nightclub's main floor.

In the pool of light spilling from the sign above the door, the Major picked out the hulking forms of doormen as she descended the stairs. She pegged them as private security soldiers rather than regular bouncers. "*Two mercs at the doors*," she said into the mind-comm, without breaking stride. "*Armed and enhanced*."

"*Copy that*," Batou replied, now secure in the mind-comm's use. "*We've got it covered*."

Ladriya split off from Batou and headed for the back of Sound Business, while he continued to the front door.

A peculiar sense of déjà vu washed over the Major as she reached the bottom of the stairs. Although she had never been in the place before, having briefly shared the memories of the reprogrammed geisha, it felt like she was returning to somewhere that held horrors and darkness for her. She frowned, dismissing the thought, and looked around.

A hard-edged bass beat thumped the thick air of the club where it issued out of tall speaker stacks across the room. Holographic strippers took up some airspace; several holo wrestling matches were also on view, drawing cheers and wagers. Knots of gruff men sat in booths on shiny vinyl couches clustered around private tables half-hidden by screens. They all bore the colors of the local gangster crews, the nubs of yakuza tattoos visible around their wrists or poking out from their starched shirt collars. Hostess synthetics in plastic outfits flitted back and forth between the groups, bringing them trays of beer or cycling through false bouts of laughter at their off-color jokes. A male hologram offered some variety, asking a patron, "Or is this more your thing?"

Nearly all of the customers seemed to be armed. "*There's a lotta heat in here for a nightclub,*" the Major reported into the comm.

"*It's a yakuza club,*" Batou replied over the comm from his position outside the building. "*What did you expect? I quite like the place.*"

The Major smiled, her tone dry as she replied into the comm, "*Why am I not surprised?*"

Dancers cavorted inside transparent cubes around the stage, and as she watched, the Major saw a Caucasian girl rise up into one of them, her hands drawing shapes in the air as she gyrated seductively toward a guy who had just settled in at the rail.

Things were moving too slowly. *"I'm gonna have to draw some attention,"* the Major informed her team over the comm, *"see if I can access the basement that way."*

Even among so many attractive women, both real and synth, it wasn't difficult for the Major to get herself noticed. As she walked across the main floor, a lot of people looked her way, especially the men.

A young gangster, called Diamond Face because of the way light sparkled across his metal lower jaw, paid close attention to how the Major moved and the look of her skin. She was not the usual Sound Business customer. The combination of his mech jaw and flesh upper lip slurred his speech a little, but that was better than being knocked out every time he got punched during a bar fight. Not that he was worried about being hit by this out-of-her-depth babe while he worked out exactly what she'd had done to her. It looked special.

At the front door, Batou was stopped by the pair of bouncers and the old-fashioned accordion security gate behind them. Handsome types, pretty ladies and hatchet-faced gangsters were waved through without comment, but a guy like Batou was subject to a little more scrutiny. He sighed and allowed the bouncers to scan and frisk him, secure in the knowledge that they wouldn't find anything dangerous on him. His gaze crossed that of a tall, spindly doorman with cyber-optic eyes and what looked like ritual scars on his face. The man's enhancements were showy and definitely not legally sanctioned.

"You're not here looking for any trouble, are you?" the bouncer asked.

Batou gave his standard response. "I'm just here for the girls... and the beer."

Inside the nightclub, the Major continued across the main floor, checking out the clientele, and avoided walking through a holographic wrestling match, which was accompanied by grunts from the combatants and shouts from the viewing patrons.

Diamond Face blocked the Major's way. "Can I help you?"

The Major tried to determine if the man had been part of what she'd seen in the Deep Dive. "I'm looking for someone."

"You been here before?" Diamond Face asked. He looked her up and down appreciatively.

"My friend had some mech work done here," the Major said. The statement seemed credible enough, given what she already knew of the place. "Industry stuff."

"We don't do mech work here," Diamond Face insisted.

This was an outright lie, but the Major chose not to confront him. "My mistake." She turned to walk away, but found another gangster blocking her path.

Diamond Face gave her his most inviting grin, which was fairly repulsive. "Why don't you come have fun with us? We'll have some privacy."

This would allow access to hidden parts of the club, which was why the Major was here, so she did her best to look receptive.

Admitted to the club, Batou was walking its warren of hallways. He passed a table where another bouncer, heavily armed, was watching the same holo-wrestling match that was rumbling along in the main room.

Batou tuned out the wrestlers' grunts so that he could focus on Major, coming in over the comms to tell him, "*I'm in.*"

In the main room, a sexy woman propositioned a male patron. This seemed to be the primary female/male dynamic here, sellers and buyers, though there were a few couples that might be genuine dates.

The Major allowed Diamond Face to escort her to the private VIP space. It was small—someone would have to work hard to avoid bumping into other people in here—with blue leather upholstered walls, red leather couches and a stripper pole to one side. The Major had been in her share of dodgy establishments since joining the Section, but this was perhaps the worst she'd ever seen in terms of pure bad taste.

A man known to his associates as Tony stood

just inside the doorway, his eyes bright with interest behind his big steel-framed glasses. The skin on his face was as shiny and synthetic as his blue suit, making him look as though the front half of his head was covered in the kind of plastic cling wrap used by the working class for leftovers. Perhaps he had had repairs done after being badly burned or suffering from a disfiguring disease; perhaps he just thought it made him appear cool and distinctive. The Major thought it made him look profoundly unhealthy.

They were joined by another member of the club's management, beefy and bald-headed, with a mouth full of metal teeth. He was known at the club as No Pupils. His eye implants were perfectly round, with unnaturally blue irises and pupils that didn't work correctly, neither dilating nor contracting in any kind of light. He also stared intently at the Major.

While the Major was still assessing the two men, Diamond Face moved with surprising speed to handcuff her wrist to the stripper pole. She let out a gasp and pulled at it experimentally, testing the strength of the metal as she made a show of trying to free herself. She didn't have to pretend that much. The cuff was dense, case-hardened steel and she wasn't going to get it off easily.

No Pupils closed the door that led back to the club. Then he leered at the Major and let out a malevolent chuckle.

Batou, unaware of the Major's current straits,

said into the comm, "*I'll be here when you need me.*" He was not worried when the Major didn't reply; she was doubtless busy seeking evidence of what she'd seen in her Deep Dive.

The men's room was just around the corner, past a couple of out of order vu-phones and the stuttering hologram display of a cigarette machine. Inside, it reeked of stale beer and spilled piss, and Batou took a breath through his mouth. A shapely pre-operative transgender patron was relieving herself at one of the urinals. Like Diamond Face, she too sported a metal lower jaw, the house modification specialty.

Batou tried to avoid making eye contact. He couldn't risk starting a conversation that might keep her in the room with him and he definitely didn't want the lady to think he was making a pass at her.

In the private room, the club boss Tony, sweating excessively and reeking of what passed for top-shelf liquor in Sound Business, leaned in close to the Major. "You say your friend worked here?"

Either Tony had misunderstood Diamond Face, or Diamond Face had misunderstood the Major. Or else she'd been made as law enforcement and they were toying with her. But the Major stuck to her story. "I said my friend *had* work done here."

"She's human… your 'friend'?" Tony sounded at once playful and threatening, implying the Major had really been talking about herself. His words also implied that he perceived far more about the Major's nature than made her comfortable.

She stalled for time. "Now what's that supposed to mean?" she said aloud, carefully shifting her weight, so that she was braced for whatever might come next. She reached out over the mind-comm. "*Batou.*" There was no response. She tried again. "*Can you hear me?*"

Tony leaned in still closer to inspect her, his sweat dripping and his smell even worse. "Mmm, who did this... stunning work on you?" he murmured, stroking the Major's hair. "It's divine." No one should be able to tell simply from looking at her that the Major had any work done at all. That this man was able to detect anything of her true nature suggested there was military-grade scanning tech hidden either in the room or perhaps somewhere in that absurd shiny blue suit.

Tony's fingers began to descend from her hair to her cleavage. The Major grabbed his hand to stop him, but No Pupils jabbed her with an electric prod. A crackling sizzle of current made her jerk against the pole as the voltage coursed through her. Overload discharges sparked from her joints and at the corner of her vision, warning icons blinked red as her cyber-systems felt the effects of the voltage.

The Major struggled to hold herself up, and abruptly the shocks halted as the thug lifted the baton. Her body continued to shake as her artificial nerve pathways cycled through a reset.

No Pupils chuckled softly, enjoying her reaction.

In the men's room, the other patron was taking so long that Batou thought he'd look like some kind of voyeur if he continued to just stand there, so he finally took his place at another urinal and used it. At last, the trans woman left. Satisfied that he was alone, Batou called out on the mind-comm. "*Ladriya? Guns.*"

Ladriya's response was prompt. The bathroom's transom window opened inward from the street and a machine gun slipped through the opening into Batou's hand. He tucked the weapon inside his voluminous coat.

"*Here,*" Ladriya said over the comm, letting Batou know she was still in position outside in the alley.

In the VIP room, Tony circled around the Major. She twitched, aiming to look like a cyber-augmented but fully human woman who had just been subjected to a debilitating electric shock, and reached out again on the comm. "*Batou… I'm losing signal.*"

There was still no response from her teammate but, unfortunately, there was another voice in her ear as Tony put his mouth right next to it and whispered, "Don't worry, sweetie. We have privacy."

Privacy? The Major wondered if he meant more than the closed door, if Tony knew about the mind-comms. His next words confirmed it. "Listen. No signals going in or out."

The Major trembled and inhaled sharply.

There didn't seem any point in lingering in the

men's room now that he had his gun, so Batou emerged and headed for the bar. He spoke again over the comm. "*Major, I'm in position. Do you copy?*" There was no response. By now, Batou was starting to worry but he was also face to face with the bartender, a fit, bare-chested fellow covered in tattoos, with a right-eye implant and a pure dark mech left arm. From his glowering expression, he clearly was not among the legion of bartenders famed for being good listeners.

Batou decided not to even try questioning the guy; no good could come of it. "Beer," he ordered. While the bartender retrieved a bottle, Batou used the mind-comm again, this time trying for dry humor. "*If you don't answer, you're gonna hurt my feelings.*" No answer.

The bartender thumped the bottle down in front of Batou and opened it, giving the Section Nine soldier an inhospitable glare as he did so.

Batou took a swig of the beer, which tasted like it had been recycled, and glared back at the bartender. With no response from the Major, he tried an alternative. "*Ladriya, do you have Major on comms?*"

Ladriya came through clearly on the comms, but her reply was not comforting. "*Got nothing. Signal's still blocked.*"

In the VIP room, No Pupils struck the Major again with the electric prod. She couldn't stop herself from flailing against the pole, chained there by the handcuff. Sparks tumbled about her and she fell to her knees, her breath trembling. She was thankful that at least Tony stepped away from her, taking his smell and sweat to an almost safe distance, taking a seat on the red leather sofa that ringed the walls.

"I'm afraid I get bored rather easily, so..." Tony paused for effect. "If you don't want to talk..." He paused again and began tapping his foot to the beat of the music pulsing through the walls from the main room. "Maybe you wanna dance!" He hissed rhythmically in time with the taps of his foot and began shaking his shoulders to the music in a manic shimmy.

No Pupils giggled, swallowed, and jabbed Major with the electric prod again. He gave a cry of pure excitement as she jerked and gasped.

Still at the bar, Batou was getting impatient and anxious. He didn't like either of those emotions, so he was shoving them down in favor of growing anger as he spoke into the comms once more. "*Major, come on. Answer me.*"

He couldn't help noticing that yakuza enforcers at a number of tables were staring at him suspiciously. As a holographic stripper beckoned, her words indistinct, the two bouncers who'd let Batou in earlier approached him from behind, one of them jabbing a pistol into his ribs.

Batou exhaled and inhaled, irritated. He turned to the bouncer who had cautioned him at the front door and used the man's words against him. "I thought you said no trouble."

In the private room, No Pupils cried out with joy as he continued to jab Major with the prod. Tony made boom-box vocalizations, boogying to the beat pulsing in from the club's sound system.

The Major gave another agonized gasp, arousing her tormentors even further.

"Dance," Tony told her. He continued to sigh and click along with the music as he danced toward the Major.

"Ah-ha!" No Pupils shrieked with laughter.

The Major's gasps became louder, her trembling more violent.

"Ah-seeeee..." Tony was now trying to sing along with the music, sounding as though he was building to some sort of ecstatic climax.

"Mmm... no," the Major quivered.

"Eeeeee..." Tony's singing got even stranger.

"Enough." The Major's voice shook.

Tony was so giddily delighted to hear his captive beg that he stopped dancing to listen to her and started chortling.

"The truth is..." the Major went on, marshaling her strength. She would only get one shot at this.

"Mmm," Tony encouraged her.

She fought down the tremors and slid both arms up to grip the pole above her, and then all the vulnerability, all the fear and panic melted off her expression and left a wicked smile in their place. "... I wasn't built to dance," the Major concluded. She took a moment to savor the gangsters' reactions, then leapt up and flipped in mid-air, descending to kick No Pupils in the head. Then she swung herself inverted on the pole, her feet pressing to the ceiling as No Pupils sent another charge into the space where she had been an instant before. Sparks flew, but he had no time to react as she spun and whirled around the pole, planting both feet in his chest and kicking him back into the sofa with a freight-train blow.

Diamond Face uttered a mechanical-sounding growl through his enhanced jaw. Tony seemed too far gone to appreciate that the tables had turned. He laughed and clapped as the Major flipped back onto her feet, kicking Diamond Face. Even his gasp of pain sounded mechanical. The Major kicked him again, snarling.

She turned to Tony, unleashing a flurry of punches that sent him reeling back toward the door. Tony emitted an "Ooh!" of pain, but even then, the Major was afraid he might be enjoying himself.

No Pupils recovered sufficiently to lunge, knife in hand. The Major ducked out of range as Tony fell out the open door into the bar.

Most of the patrons were startled and alarmed, but Batou was relieved to see the Major through the doorway. He reeled back, head-butted one of the bouncers and smashed the beer bottle over the other one's head. The man staggered back, trying to dash beer and broken glass out of his face.

The other bouncer now swung his fist, still holding the pistol. Batou easily blocked the blow and grabbed the bouncer's gun hand, shoving it aside. The revolver went off with a loud, flat bang, blowing through the torso of the man Batou had hit with the beer bottle, and sent him tumbling to the floor. Batou wrenched the shooter's gun arm around with both hands, slamming it against the bar with an agonizing snap of breaking bone.

Every patron in the Sound Business nightclub took notice. Nearly all of them were members of one kind of criminal fraternity or another. As one, the gangsters put down their drinks and turned toward Batou, while the civilian patrons screamed and ran for cover.

The bartender grabbed a gun from under the counter. Batou, still gripping the armed bouncer's hand, slammed it down on the bar, causing the other man's gun to shoot the bartender.

"Oww!" the bouncer cried.

And all hell broke loose.

Batou, seeing a pair of gangsters taking aim at him, turned the bouncer's hand so that his pistol took out the two yakuza before they could fire. Behind him, the bartender uttered a few dying groans.

The Major was still in the private room. She wanted to help Batou, but she was still handcuffed to the stripper's pole and still fighting No Pupils. He came at her and she punched him in the face. He yelled.

The sounds of the private room fight were entirely swallowed up by the commotion in the main bar as people shouted, yelled, shrieked and either tried to run or find shelter, or else figure out who they ought to kill.

Batou, settling on two more gangsters, used the bouncer's hand still clamped around the pistol to shoot them both.

Diamond Face rejoined the fight in the back room, pulling a pistol. The Major grabbed his arm at the same time she redirected a knife strike by No Pupils, meant for her neck, into Diamond Face. The man groaned in agony, clutching himself where he'd been stabbed. No Pupils grabbed the Major by the throat, but she threw a hard elbow into his face, using his weight against him so that he lost his balance and went down.

At the bar, Batou snatched the pistol completely free of the bouncer's hand and shot him, then kicked him down into a conversation pit, knocking down two more gangsters who'd been preparing to open fire.

"Get outside!" yelled one of the more sensible patrons. Many in the crowd stampeded for the exits. In the rising chaos, Batou spotted another pair of gangsters targeting him and shot them as well.

The Major used another powerful kick to send the groaning No Pupils staggering back away from her. Then she hurled Diamond Face out through the door and onto the barroom floor.

Batou looked down to see a sorry, unconscious mess of a guy with a cracked metal jaw. He didn't know what the out-cold criminal had done to deserve the thrashing he most obviously had received, but he guessed it had something to do with underestimating the Major. That tended to happen. People looked at her and didn't see the soldier she was, they only saw what they wanted to see, what they thought she was. Generally, it didn't end well.

He didn't have much time to reflect on this, though, because those goons who hadn't died or run off kept shooting at him. Batou dropped the bouncer's pistol and pulled out the machine gun he'd hidden under his coat. The weapon was almost the size of his torso, which made it a little unwieldy, but it had terrific punch, and it couldn't be beat for tackling a hostile crowd.

In the private room, No Pupils pulled out a pistol. The Major was surprised it had taken him this long to try a firearm, but her speed was much better than his aim, and all his shots at her went wild. Then she kicked his gun arm up into the air. He screamed.

In the barroom, a yakuza armed with two guns gave an attack yell. This was a poor tactic, as it alerted Batou to the yakuza's intention and position and allowed him to shoot first. The gangster fell back with a dying groan, his guns tilting upward so that their shots punctured the ceiling.

No Pupils tried to shoot the Major once more. She easily swung around the stripper's pole, gained footing on the wall and ran around it at a ninety-degree angle to the floor as she evaded the bullets, then kicked No Pupils in the head. He dropped onto his face, insensate.

With no one left to fight, the Major took a moment to catch her breath.

Out in the club, only one gangster still seemed inclined to fight. He charged at Batou with a battle cry worthy of his warrior forebears. Batou frantically brought up his gun and fired. The gangster dropped mid-charge with a dying grunt that overlapped with the grunting holographic wrestlers and the sighs of the holographic strippers.

Tony was bleeding out, his breath coming in raspy exhalations. The Major got the handcuff key out of his pocket and released herself from the pole. Taking out her pistol, she walked into the club. As she did, she could feel the comms come back on, no longer blocked by the tech shielding the back room.

"*Back on comms*," the Major told her team. "*I'm heading to the back room.*"

Batou tried to keep his reply light, but he knew he probably sounded as relieved as he felt. "*I missed ya. I'll meet you there.*"

The Major scrambled down a damp stone staircase, deeper and deeper into the club's gloomy lower levels. Once more she felt that strange stab of alien recollection, a fragment of the geisha synthetic's memory merging with her perception of the moment.

The stairs opened out into a narrow, ill-lit basement corridor lined with rusty metal lockers. The Major recognized the closed door at the hallway's end from her Deep Dive. It was stained dark with something that could have been old grease or dried blood.

She kicked the door open, but was brought up short. The ground underfoot suddenly changed from old, cool concrete to something uneven and overly hot. She stumbled, thrown off her gait. In front of her was the pagoda she'd seen at the intersection, when she'd glitched earlier. Only now the pagoda was in flames, showering her with scraps of burning timber.

The Major was disconcerted by the vision. It looked real. Worse, it *felt* real, like a terrible loss that she could not comprehend. The pagoda vanished.

In the pagoda's place, framed in the gloom, she saw a shrouded figure, a man perhaps, a hood rendering his face invisible in the dimness, the black fall of a cape coming off his shoulders and outlining the rest of him in vague lines of shadow. He almost blended in with the ashes and rubble. He rose to his feet and said to the Major what he'd previously said through the geisha bot. "Collaborate with Hanka Robotics and be destroyed."

It was Kuze. The Major unhesitatingly sent three bullets into his chest, but they had no effect. Kuze melted away into digital rectangles, before disappearing entirely. He hadn't been there at all. She'd been fooled by a hologram. Frustrated, the Major lowered her gun.

"Major?" Batou shouted from the hallway. He'd heard the shots and burst into the work room ready for combat, but saw she was alone. "Hey."

Seeing the dispirited look on her face, Batou put a comforting hand on the Major's shoulder. She might have said something about Kuze, but she was distracted by a beeping noise, the kind made by a smoke alarm, or a timer.

The Major looked around. A number of tall metal cylinders were mounted along one of the walls. On closer examination, the Major thought these might be oxygen canisters. Each cylinder was equipped with a red light that blinked in time with the beeps. And on each one of the cylinders was a high-explosive grenade on a timer, jerry-rigged and primed to explode.

The Major's first reaction was a gasp of dismay. She burst into motion, yelling and shoving Batou through the gloomy space back into the hallway, but it was too late. Inside the room, the grenades detonated with a massive concussion, obliterating everything within, bringing down the ceiling. A swirling rush of smoke and shrapnel mushroomed outward, blowing the Major and Batou down the corridor, the fire rolling over them. Batou screamed, clutching at his seared eyes. Then thundering darkness consumed them both.

5

HUMAN ERROR

Another stark transition occurred, from choking blackness to bright, blazing white light.

In one instant, the Major was being smothered by the dark, enveloping debris, and in the next, she was lying atop an operating table, bathed in the glow of sensor webs and scanning modules. She blinked, fatigue indicators flickering and dying at the edge of her vision. Her neural linkages cycled through their reboot sequence and she was aware once again of the world around her.

She forced away her dismay at the abrupt sense of dislocation and refocused. She was in Dr. Ouelet's biomimetic lab at Hanka, being repaired. Her first instinct was to rise up, but an apparatus exactly like a ten-times-larger copy of the one that had mended her wrist was arched over her, its tools steadily working on her entire body. Her torso was open chest to hips, most of the synthetic organs and implants damaged in some way and pulsing variously blood red, white and black. There was nothing left of her right leg except the metal pole that formed its core, and her left thigh was open to its foundation. She could see Dr. Ouelet through the observation glass in her office one room over, working at a console to direct the repair machinery.

"Where's Batou?" the Major asked. She dreaded what the answer might be.

But Ouelet's reply over the intercom was reassuring. "In Enhancement, next door. He's doing well." She added with motherly reproach, "*You* took most of the blast."

The brief surge of fear that had threatened to well up in the Major's chest fell back and faded away. She had been in this place and this situation before, more than once, and Ouelet was always there to put her back together. Still, she frowned, looking inward as her internal systems diagnostics brought up a dozen error readings. Her dermal plates were visible, much of the artificial skin badly shredded, torn ragged as if by the claws of some great beast. Internal circuitry in her limbs and torso showed in many places, exposed to the air. She wanted to get back to work at once, but it was going to take hours to apply a new layer of skin and for the hardware to reset.

"I saw him down there." The Major needed Ouelet to understand how Kuze had toyed with her and that it was essential she be back on the case as soon as possible, even though it was hard to put definite meaning to the events in the club's basement. "It was like…" she paused momentarily, "he waited to see me."

"We synaptic-scanned you," Ouelet said over the intercom, anticipating the Major's concern. "Everything you witnessed went to Section Nine to evaluate." She paused before adding, "You know, the scan… also turned up a number of glitches."

"They've been getting worse," the Major admitted.

"Since when?"

"Since the Deep Dive."

Ouelet left her office and entered the operating room to stand by the Major's bedside. "Do any of the glitches mean something to you?"

"No," the Major said, with more surety than she felt. "They don't."

Ouelet took a moment before speaking again. "You've been inside the same shell as he has." The Major's Deep Dive had been within the geisha's cyber-consciousness, which had also been entered and probed previously by Kuze. "That could have… very serious consequences."

The Major could hardly argue with this, so she said nothing.

"You were not authorized to Deep Dive the geisha," Ouelet reproved.

"You're disappointed." The Major felt regret.

There were few people whose opinions she valued, but Ouelet was one of them.

"No," Ouelet corrected her, "I'm worried." She swallowed. "You're not invulnerable. I can repair your body, but I can't protect your mind."

This didn't make sense. "Why not?" the Major queried. "You can see all my thoughts, so you should be able to secure them."

Rather than answering directly, Ouelet turned the conversation to a theme she often visited—that the Major had a responsibility to exercise self-preservation. "Try and understand your importance, Mira." Ouelet paused, then added, "You're what everyone will become one day."

The Major didn't wish that day on anyone. Meanwhile, Ouelet's words simply reinforced that there were no others like the Major, that there might never be others in her lifetime. "You don't know how alone that makes me feel."

Eventually, Ouelet released her and the Major dressed stiffly in her spare clothes, the surface of her mended skin still pale and moist where it was setting into place. Fluid link replacements in her joint servos repaired the damage she had suffered from the electroshocks and, as much as was possible, she felt whole again. The visions in the murky room, the explosion and the engulfing wave of dust—those things were fading already, as if they were someone else's memories that she had only heard about.

She made her way across the hall to the Enhancement Department, slowing as she approached, a fraction of doubt forcing its way into her thoughts.

He lost his eyes? Batou had come down to that basement looking for her, and if he had been badly wounded, she bore some responsibility for it.

She saw Batou through the window of a recovery room. He was sitting up, his left shoulder and arm secured by a speed-heal wrap that held broken bones in place and allowed the replacement skin to take hold without risk of infection. His eyes were covered by a protective VR headset.

"I can see you out there, you know." Batou raised his voice to make sure the Major heard him.

She raised her middle finger in response, her voice dry. "How many fingers am I holding up?"

Batou smacked his lips. "Funny." His tone was sarcastic, as if the Major had done something childish, but they both knew how glad he was that she was there.

The Major entered the recovery room, and Batou opened up the headset to reveal what was underneath. After what she'd been told, she was expecting it, but it was still a shock when the medical module around his face folded open and Batou looked up at her. His kind eyes were gone, and she stifled a small gasp of dismay. From the side, it looked as though two short, flesh-colored gun barrels had been implanted in his eye sockets. Moving to look at him straight on, the Major saw that Batou's implants contained multi-layered cyber-mech lenses; the inside workings of each new eye bore a resemblance to a telescope, and had the function to match. They rotated and focused on her as she approached. The technicians had managed to replicate the blue of his original irises in the optical discs that now sat at the end of his eye barrels, which just made his appearance more unsettling.

Batou had a notion of how he looked. "Say something nice," he requested.

The Major liked him too much to lie, so she went with an insult and a smirk. "You chose those?"

Batou grinned. "They're tactical." This was true—there was no such thing as too much enhancement for a Section Nine agent.

"Always for the job," the Major teased.

Batou shrugged and then winced. "What else I got?"

She didn't want to discuss the fact that neither of them had lives outside of their work. So she said something nice after all. "They suit you."

"Yeah?" Batou sounded hopeful. He'd gone for the full military package. "I got night vision, mile-zoom... and X-ray." He gave the Major a sly grin. "I guess I see like you now."

If that was true, the Major thought, Batou was in for a hell of a learning curve. "Don't worry, you'll get used to it."

Batou swallowed. He knew it would make her uncomfortable, but he still had to say it. "Thanks for saving my ass."

He didn't expect a reaction, nor did he get one. What the Major really wanted to ask was whether he'd seen anything strange in the club—a burning pagoda, perhaps, or Kuze's cloaked image. But surely he'd say so if he had, and she didn't want to bring up anything that might make a colleague, even Batou, think there might be something wrong with her perceptions.

"Glad to see you're okay," the Major said, and headed for the door.

"Major?" Batou called. She stopped. "Could you feed the dogs for me? I don't want to scare them."

So underneath the bluster, Batou was afraid his new look was disturbing. The Major didn't know how to counter that, so she just nodded and said, "Any time."

Batou's self-doubt was sincere but contained. After the Major left, he spotted a pretty worker seated at a console in the recovery room. He zoomed in on her with his new eyes, delighted by how well they worked and what they were showing him.

That night, the Major went to the alley where Batou had taken her previously. She had a bag full of butcher's scraps, but this time, the only dog to come out of the shadows was the basset hound mix Gabriel.

He trotted up to her, tail wagging, and whined to be petted even after she'd put the meat down for him.

The Major knelt. At first, she wore the frown that was her usual resting expression. The little dog was happy with the attention. He didn't care whether she was fully biological or in a synthetic shell, he just wanted the touch of a friendly hand, a friendly face to look into. That, she supposed, was what it meant to be human. Or in this instance, canine. She put her hand on Gabriel and smiled at him. The dog wagged his tail again.

A much less pleasant interaction was taking place in Aramaki's office at Section Nine headquarters. The chief was alone with Cutter, who wore an expensive dark green silk suit; Aramaki was dressed in a grey three-piece ensemble that made him look frailer than he was.

For the most part, Section Nine was Aramaki's kingdom, but the reality was that Cutter pulled many of the strings that kept the unit in operation. The Hanka CEO was the living juncture where police work and public security intersected with commerce and politics. His presence in Aramaki's office was significant.

Cutter's words were measured, but there was no disguising the fury behind them. "Are you insufficiently funded, Mr. Aramaki? Is Section Nine missing some critical resource?"

The CEO knew exactly how well funded Section Nine was. Aramaki did not rise to the bait. He replied in Japanese, "We have everything that we require."

"Major is our most sophisticated weapon..." Cutter allowed himself a brief smile of admiration, "only if she's intact." In the next instant, he became accusatory, glaring at Aramaki. "And Dr. Ouelet informed me that you let her dive into a corrupted geisha." Cutter still couldn't believe that something so irresponsible, so foolhardy, so potentially disastrous had been done. Aramaki could have risked anyone on the team and spared Hanka's single most valuable asset.

She'd been connected to work, malware, viruses, trapdoors, glitches, and implants. If she was compromised, if Kuze had put code inside her, that would change everything. The Major was the prototype of the perfect soldier. If she was vulnerable to hacking and it got out, the reputation of Hanka Robotics might never recover.

Aramaki didn't bother to point out that he had not authorized the Major's Deep Dive. He took full responsibility for any actions undertaken by his subordinates, whether he'd sanctioned them or not. Also, it would be shameful of him to do or say anything that might cause Cutter to take it upon himself to chastise the Major directly. That was not Cutter's place, but he would not see it that way. Men like Cutter never did.

Oblivious to what Aramaki was thinking, Cutter continued with his lecture. "You realize the supreme importance that Hanka represents to this government. Major is the future of my company. If you compromise her systems again, I will *burn* this section."

Aramaki gave Cutter the formal bow that a subordinate gave to a man of greater social stature. "Yes, sir. Mr. Cutter." He paused. "But be careful who you threaten. I answer to the prime minister, not to Hanka."

The giant digital ads continued to rule the skies of New Port City, even at night. "Digital democracy," one proclaimed. "Enjoy your life again."

A male sports announcer revealed, "And in Contouren ball today, the Mangorea continue their quest for their third Contouren cup in..."

A commercial jingle, an earworm that was the bane of all who heard it, sang out, "Playpod time, Playpod time..."

In her apartment, the Major examined herself in a holographic mirror, running her fingers over her cheek and lips, trying to feel whether she could distinguish them from normal flesh, whether she could recall if the sensations she experienced now were different from those she had known before the shell. But she couldn't remember.

The Major had been to the city's red light district dozens of times on missions. Now, though, she was here as a civilian. She wandered through the teeming bazaars and the alleys of the night market. The activity there never ended, only changed, with one set of vendors and hawkers moving on for the day and a different crowd coming in for the hours after sunset.

A chill ran through her, and even though she knew it was only an emulation running from her biological brain to her machine-form body, it felt *real*. Suddenly, all that the Major wanted was to remember and to experience a *connection*.

The holographic ads in this neighborhood promised every kind of sexual experience possible. "No matter what your interest," a female voice announced seductively over a billboard, "we have it all. Virtual to real, all partner robots are anatomically sound, sterile, and can be customized to your liking."

On the ground, a human prostitute shouted obscenities at a geisha bot, trying to get her to relinquish her patch of sidewalk turf.

A male announcer promised, "Perform when the time comes—we'll kill all your worries goodbye. New triozide bull formula gives you a natural..."

A corner prostitute noticed the Major and beckoned. "Come here! With me!"

The Major continued on, moving further into the night. Overhead, another talking holo-ad suggested, "Create your own beauty. Beauty enhanced."

And there, in a doorway, was beauty. A particularly exotic-looking prostitute was leaning there, tall and athletic, in her early twenties. The Major could see how she was attempting to compete for clients with the synthetics by adopting the same style of clothes, the same kind of elaborate shiny make-up that recalled the circular face of a porcelain doll.

But something about her made the Major stop and walk over to her.

"You human?" the Major asked.

The prostitute was not offended. "Yeah."

The woman's name was Lia and she had no objection to going to the Major's apartment. The two women sat down between the corrugated walls of the sleeping alcove, facing each other. Weak illumination played over their features. Their gestures were halting and tentative. The Major felt as if she was being carried along by a need that had long been buried in her, awakened now by something distant and bright. She understood that she was hardly the kind of client Lia catered to usually, but Lia seemed to have all the patience in the world.

"Can you take that off?" The Major indicated the decorative rounded make-up patterned over Lia's face, the fake aspect that made her appear less human and more synthetic. "So I can see your face."

Lia's expression suggested that this was a request she had not heard before, but she was happy to comply. The Major watched in silent fascination as the make-up peeled from the other woman in a second, dead plastic skin. Lia detached the round, slick patch that encircled the lower portion of her face. Her glossy, over-colored lips faded back to their normal shade, looking much softer without their lipstick shield. Lia reached up and stripped away false, cartoonishly long eyelashes, self-consciously running a hand over her shorn scalp, smoky with a fuzz of hair. Moment by moment, the other woman brought herself back to her essential human nature.

Their skins were a study in contrast. Where the Major's flesh was pale, and almost reflective, Lia's ochre tones were wonderfully freckled and authentic.

The Major moved closer, reaching up to stroke Lia's cheek, then ran her thumb over Lia's lip. She saw the young woman react in surprise to her touch. "What does that feel like?"

"It feels…" Lia hesitated, "…different."

The Major ran a finger under Lia's eye, then stroked her cheek again. It evoked a memory, though no names or faces came with it. But there had been breath, and smell, and skin, and warmth.

Lia exhaled very softly, nervous. "What are you?" she asked. Was that fear in her eyes?

The Major did not reply.

6

GHOST HACK

Even though she lived in a far more elegant part of town that could only be afforded by politicians, top executives and corporate scientists, Dr. Sonia Dahlin's apartment was not extensively furnished. Like most Hanka personnel, she didn't spend much time in her personal dwelling. Tonight, though, she had taken her current project home with her and was up late, working. She could have remained in the lab, and protocol dictated that she should, but by the end of the regular workday, she had desperately needed a nap, a shower and a change of clothes in that order. There were places to sleep and even wash up at the Hanka Tower, of course, but she didn't have a clean shirt with her and the thought of having to go on working with her own sweat clinging to her was more than Dahlin could take today.

Moreover, Dahlin felt uneasy on this project. She

had been directed to find every last bit of information that could be excavated from the geisha bot's systems, but with all of the scientists who'd been killed in their laboratories or semi-public settings, it seemed safer to work from home at night, getting in before dark and not venturing out again until dawn.

So here she was in her living room, rested, clean, with a cigarette dangling from her mouth, overflowing ashtray at hand. The hacked geisha bot was spread out on a table before her, with a hologram reading SECURE—PROJECT 2571 hovering in the air. In smaller words, the hologram also read, ENCRYPTED FOLDER STRUCTURE—DR. OSMOND.

Dahlin scanned a hologram of the geisha's head in order to access the encrypted file folder that the bot had hacked from Osmond. She reached out and manipulated the hologram to decrypt it.

The decryption brought forth a new hologram: HANKA—PERSONNEL FILES.

Dahlin frowned. Someone had gone to a lot of trouble—not to mention expense, bribery, and murder—for a directory that could have been obtained in far easier, less bloody ways. What information was in here that was so important?

There were armed doormen downstairs in case of intruders and Dahlin always set the lock code on her door as soon as she stepped inside. There was no reason for her to fear that someone might break in, and consequently no reason for her to be on alert. So, as the scientist poured through the data streams, she did not notice her front door opening silently.

But then a shadow moved where no shadow should be, and Dahlin turned to see Kuze standing right behind her. She could only see a glimpse of his face, pale beneath the hood.

Kuze reached out and plucked the lit cigarette from Dahlin's trembling lips. She was terrified, but not paralyzed by it. Her hands were still on her console, and she palmed the thumb drive from it, causing the holograms to disappear.

Kuze didn't seem to care about that. "Look at me," he commanded.

Dahlin peered at his face under the hood. Her own features registered revulsion and pity.

"Tell me what they took from me," Kuze continued.

She knew he was referring to the scientists of Hanka. She even knew what he was talking about. But Kuze was here for vengeance, and probably nothing she could say would dissuade him. Still, Dahlin tried, the words coming out in a frightened gasp. "I'm sorry. They never told us."

Kuze's reply came in a gesture rather than speech. With one hand, he broke the detachable eye-plate off of Dahlin's face, blinding her and revealing the quik-ports underneath.

As Dahlin screamed with pain and terror, Kuze tossed her eye-plate aside and rammed his hand into the ports in her eye sockets.

* * *

The next day, Batou was at the wheel of his car, the Major riding shotgun beside him. "It feels weird driving with these eyes," Batou said. He expected some sort of smartass rejoinder, but when he glanced at the Major, he saw she was busy applying medication to one of the quik-ports in her neck. "Why do you take that?" He'd never asked before, but the eye implants made him feel like he'd earned the right; he had much more in common with the Major now.

She didn't object to the question. "It keeps my brain from rejecting this body."

Batou nodded. He was still on anti-rejection drugs for his eye implants; something as extensive as what had been done to the Major likely required a lifelong medication regimen.

He was about to say something, but then the car's comm lit up with Togusa's voice.

"Major, Batou... you need to get here."

"What do you got?" Batou replied into the comm. Togusa sounded grim. "Another Hanka scientist has been found dead. It's Dahlin."

Batou inhaled sharply and saw the look of alarm on the Major's face. "Got it." He jerked the steering wheel, putting the car in a one-eighty-degree spin.

When the Major and Batou arrived at Dahlin's

apartment building, Togusa, Ishikawa, Ladriya and Borma had just arrived and were waiting in the hall.

"Major, this way," Togusa directed. He led her and Batou past a murdered guard and into Dahlin's apartment. The scientist's body was on the floor.

The Major pulled back the plastic tarp covering the corpse to see Dahlin's ruined face. With the eye-plate removed and her head circuitry smashed beyond repair, Dahlin resembled a broken cyborg, even though she had been human.

One of Dahlin's hands was clenched tight. The Major's first thought was that it was a result of rigor mortis but Dahlin's other hand was open. The Major pried open Dahlin's curled fingers, trying not to snap them, and found the thumb drive clutched in the dead woman's hand.

The killer had left Dahlin's computer intact, so the Major inserted the thumb drive there. The hologram she had seen just before her death (SECURE—PROJECT 2571/ENCRYPTED FOLDER STRUCTURE—DR. OSMOND) appeared once more.

"What is that?" Togusa voiced what they were all wondering.

"She found what Kuze stole from Osmond," the Major surmised. She scanned through the personnel files, and saw highlighted within the hologram: PERSONNEL #2605, PERSONNEL #1203, PERSONNEL #2605, PERSONNEL #1502.

The Major recognized what the data revealed.

"It's a list of everyone who worked on a project called 2571." She opened the PERSONNEL #1502 file. The holograms became a succession of portraits of Hanka scientists, with identifying captions beneath the images: Dr. Houser, Dr. Osmond, Dr. Sato, Dr. Markum, Dr. Dahlin. "That's who he's targeting."

"Is anyone else on the list?" Togusa asked.

The Major scrolled past Dahlin's portrait. The next image to come up was Dr. Genevieve Ouelet.

She felt as though she'd been injected with ice water. "Find Ouelet," the Major ordered. "Now!"

Ladriya tried to contact Ouelet on her comm, with no luck. "She's in transit. Her comms are down."

A green electric truck, grubby with months of dirt, sat idling in an alleyway, its wide bulk almost filling the passage. The six-wheeler resembled a giant pill-bug. Right now, it was idling in place while its occupants ate lunch, because if there was one thing Bearded Man and Skinny Man agreed on, it was that there was no such thing as an emergency rush in the trash collection game.

In the truck's cramped and sweaty cab, Skinny Man was in the driver's seat. He was wound tight with nervous, unspent energy, even while putting noodles in his mouth and talking around them, the implant in his right temple bobbing as he went on. "I'm looking at her and I'm thinking, 'You want me to pay for violin, too?' Don't get me wrong. I love that kid to pieces. I do. 'Cause she's amazing." His words came out muffled as he chewed. "But when she practices that thing, it is painful, right?"

Bearded Man just nodded and took a bite of his own noodles, trying to avoid dropping them on his orange overalls.

Skinny Man hadn't been expecting a reply anyway. "Why not piano?"

Both men would have been astonished to know their conversation was being monitored. In the underground bunker, Kuze listened in and previewed the truck's route via his cables, waiting for the right moment.

"I mean," Skinny Man went on, "it's the same price, you know? And doesn't sound so bad." He took another bite of his noodles. "At least if you can't play that proper..." Suddenly, lights began to circulate within his implant. His speech slowed, "... it doesn't sound..."

His face went slack and blank-eyed, and he became unnaturally motionless. His eyelids gave a peculiar flutter. At his side, his partner's face shared the same blank emptiness. They both released their noodle containers, which dropped onto the cab floor.

Skinny Man's put both his hands on the steering wheel, as if the appendages were two separately animated things moving of their own volition. He gunned the truck's engine and it hurtled forward in a sudden rush, gaining speed as it lurched toward the mouth of the alleyway, motor roaring.

Ouelet was in the back seat of her limo, contemplating her next move as her chauffeur gracefully guided the sleek black car through the streets. Her assistant sat beside her, typing with hands that had been enhanced with ten fingers each. This gave the assistant a slightly insect-like appearance from the forearms outward, but the tech was ideal for a job that required letter-perfect real-time transcription. Over the limo's sound system, opera diva Maria Callas was singing the "La mamma morta" aria from Umberto Giordano's opera *Andrea Chénier*.

Ouelet sighed. Cutter had been making his unhappiness with the Major's investigation known inside and outside of Hanka. She hoped he wouldn't really remove the Major from her supervision. That would be counter-productive.

All Ouelet's thoughts were swept away as the huge green truck suddenly smashed into the driver's side of the limo in a violent, screeching impact of twisting steel and breaking glass. The T-bone collision sent the smaller vehicle slipping away and into a sideways somersault, rolling it onto its roof before it skidded to a halt across the roadway.

The sound system, unlike the engine, was intact. Callas sang on. *"Porto sventura a chi bene mi vuole!"* *I bring misfortune to all who love me.*

Ouelet cried out. Her first thought, even before she realized how much pain she was in, even before it sank in that her life was in immediate danger, was that her surgeon's hands might have been damaged. For all that she touted enhancements for others, she prided herself on her organic skills. Outside the flipped limo, the garbage truck backed up and stopped. Neither of the men in the cab of the truck showed the slightest flicker of emotion as they reached for a threadbare bag in the footwell that contained two hooded trench coats, dully reflective covers like rain slickers, which each donned around his shoulders with rote motions. Beneath the coats were small-frame submachine guns, the kind of weapon gangbangers called a chop-n-drop. They took one each.

Silently, the two men climbed out of the truck's cab. They walked toward the upside-down limousine as the wreckage creaked and clicked, its tormented metal frame still settling.

Hanka Robotics scientist Dr. Genevieve Ouelet, on her hands and knees, crawled out of a shattered window frame on the side of the limo opposite the truck, desperately pushing ahead in a terrified crouch. She searched wildly for any kind of cover that might protect her, but the nearest wall was too far away, with nothing but open asphalt between her and the meager safety it offered.

The Hanka spokeswoman continued her holographic pitch. "...and your loved ones. Protecting your ever-evolving future. Hanka Robotics."

The limo's chauffeur, hanging upside down from his seatbelt, struggled to escape from the vehicle, in too much in shock to comprehend that there was more danger on the street than inside the wreck. Dead-eyed, Skinny Man aimed his gun and fired a quick burst into the man's belly, killing him.

Ouelet had cleared the car but was unable to stand. A shadow fell over her and she looked up, dazed, at the machine-gun muzzle pointing at her face. Holding the weapon was a skinny man wearing a trench coat, with data lights cascading through the implant on the right side of his head. He screamed, glaring down at her through dead eyes, "2571! Tell me everything!"

Then she heard the roaring snarl of an overcharged engine and both assassins pivoted toward the source of the sound. Ouelet saw a blocky, military-style jeepney hurtling toward them down the roadway, and a determined face behind the wheel.

The bigger, Bearded Man, who hadn't said anything, brought up his gun one-handed and sent a braying lance of fire toward the oncoming vehicle. Massive holes punctured the cab and the hood of the jeepney, but the heavy vehicle kept on coming until its tires blew out. It coasted jerkily forward for a few yards on sheer momentum, then creaked to a stop.

Batou's car screeched around the end of the block in a punishing turn and barreled across the intersection toward the site of the ambush. Skinny Man continued to scream at Ouelet, spittle flying from his lips. "Are you prepared to die for 257—"

The Major leapt from the car even as Batou brought it skidding to a halt. She came forward with both hands clasped around her weapon, intent on her target. She fired at Skinny Man, but the car's motion and her landing threw her aim off, and she missed. Skinny Man turned and fired back. She took cover behind the open passenger door, steadying herself. As Batou got out of the car, Skinny Man changed his aim and shot at him.

The Major didn't think—she just reacted. Leaning out from behind the open car door, and leading with her pistol, she drew a bead on Skinny Man. Her gun barked and she landed a single shot in his shoulder. It seemed to have zero effect. He returned fire again, spraying a pattern of bullets into the door.

Ladriya, Ishikawa and Togusa exited the jeepney from the back. "Go!" Togusa told Ladriya, tasking her with protecting Ouelet.

They were closing into a ring around the target, surrounding him. The Major knew that this was the critical moment.

Skinny Man abandoned Ouelet and the gunfight together. He bolted for the end of the street. His beefy partner took up the cause, exchanging fire with Ishikawa, but Skinny Man did not look back. Ouelet ducked behind the limo, putting more metal between herself and her assailant.

As he reached the end of the block, Skinny Man's free hand snapped up and activated the thermoptic function on his trench coat. Too late, the Major realized what he was wearing as his outline flickered, turned glassy—and then vanished, leaving a heat mirage distortion that receded from view altogether.

The Major ran behind the limo, simultaneously trying to protect Ouelet and bring down the shimmering outline of Skinny Man as he ran further and further out of range. Ladriya ran over to relieve the Major. "Go," Ladriya told her.

She sprang up and ran in the direction Skinny Man had taken. But the Major had no backup. Everyone else on the team was engaged in the gunfight with Bearded Man. The man did not appear to be bothered by the fact that he was outgunned and surrounded, that he'd been abandoned by his partner, or that their mission had apparently failed. He just kept firing, with no expression on his features, until two shots from Batou finally reached its target. The big man sank to his knees, then collapsed completely, dead.

Skinny Man, now blocks away, leapt down from his perch on a second-floor apartment building into a deserted alley. The surrounding buildings were grey with decay, decrepit and largely abandoned. Tattered laundry hung from a few balconies, but no faces peered out to investigate the frantic footfalls on the cement below. The man raced across the alley to a low wall at the end and scrambled up and over the barrier. Without pause, he ran down the next dismal, dirty street.

The enclosed canyons of the downtown district abruptly opened out into a flat, empty basin that reminded the Major of an ancient amphitheater. Rows of derelict tiered structures climbed away on two sides. The basin was visible but submerged beneath a foot of seawater, blown in by the last storm and just left there, as City Services never ventured into this neighborhood.

The arena-like space was much quieter than the mayhem back by the garbage truck and the wrecked limo, enough so that, even though her target was still invisible, the Major's enhanced hearing could pick out the thudding of his boots. She tracked the sound, looking for any sign of the gunman, and found ripples radiating out across the basin's shallow water, disturbed in his passing.

Thinking quickly, she went for the high ground. The Major gripped the edge of a wall and, in a few swift motions, she was up atop one of the tiers. Moving fast and low to present a smaller silhouette, she dashed along the top of the structure, still scanning the basin for the shooter. Below her, she caught sight of the gunman's footfalls in another patch of murky water. He was close.

She nodded to herself. Two could play at this game. The Major ran to the sheer drop at the edge of the tier, throwing herself into the air. In mid-drop, she triggered her own thermoptic camo, turning her into a spectral shape as she landed hard on the ground and crouched low.

She heard his footsteps come to a sudden halt—the gunman could not have missed the sound of her touchdown—and the crunch of his boots as he turned in place.

Even when cerebral cyber-enhancements are hacked to add strength and endurance, a human body has limits. The Skinny Man had reached his. He turned off the thermoptic feature on his rain coat—a cheap unit, it had been sputtering for the length of his run—and looked around.

He pivoted and saw no one, but fired his machine gun again, letting off a sustained, screaming arc of bullets that ripped through the air as he spun. He emptied the remainder of the snail-drum magazine into nothing, until the SMG's slide locked open and the steaming barrel glowed cherry-red with heat. He stormed forward, looking for a way out of the too-open space.

As if jerked away on an invisible cord, his gun was suddenly whipped out of his hand. It went spinning away to land in the water. From out of the air, or so it seemed, came a lightning-fast series of kicks and punches that cracked him across the face, drawing blood, and struck him across the chest and the back of the legs. He reeled backward, grabbing at nothing, before he fell to his knees and spat out a mouthful of thick, crimson-laced spittle. The Major, her own thermoptic suit engaged, shimmered like clear glass under water. She flipped Skinny Man into the air. He came crashing down onto his face in the shallow seawater.

He cried out in pain, but somehow still kept moving. Pulling a knife from his clothes, he slashed at the air, trying to find the Major. Instead, the Major seized his arm and twisted it, forcing him to drop the knife. She flipped him into the air again, and once more, he landed in the water.

The man was now greatly disoriented from the hack, by the blows delivered by the Major's hands, and by his skull twice connecting with the concrete under the layer of seawater. The Major grabbed him a third time, dropped him on his feet and resumed hitting him. One punch sent Skinny Man flying back through the air to land a third time face-down in the water.

Like a magic trick, the Major deactivated her thermoptic rig and was revealed, standing over him in full fury with her fists clenched. She struck out at him again in another blistering flurry of body blows and he went down hard, wheezing in pain.

He tried struggling to his feet, but she kicked him and he went down into the water anew. The Major grabbed a fistful of his soaked collar, turned him onto his back and walloped him twice in the face.

She let go of the man, but it was only to catch her breath for a moment. Then she pulled him up by the collar again. "Where's Kuze?" the Major snarled.

Skinny Man's head rolled around and he blinked, trying to focus on her. An odd change passed over his face and he flinched, staring wide-eyed at her. Before, his gaze had seemed distant and clouded. Now he was confused and afraid, as if he was a sleepwalker that had just awakened from a trance.

"Why does he want to kill Ouelet?" the Major demanded.

"I... I don't know anything!"

The Major found this unacceptable. She heard Batou running up behind her, but she ignored his approach. All the conflicted emotion she had held in check earlier now came rocketing out in the form of pure rage. She towered over the cowering man and began punching him in the face until he couldn't take any more and fell back into the water, on the verge of losing consciousness. The Major started to fish him out so she could hit him again.

Batou ran up behind her and grabbed her before she could inflict more punishment. "Enough!"

The Major glared at him.

"Enough!" Batou repeated. She shoved him but he pushed her back and stated the obvious. "We need him alive."

The Major stalked away, still furious, and Batou fished the beaten man out of the water.

* * *

Secured on a lower level of the ops center, the cube

rooms were used for interrogation of high-value targets and the kinds of enhanced criminals that the regular cops were not equipped to handle.

Skinny Man didn't think he could stand to answer the questions even one more time. "Please… I've been through this." And he had. He'd been here for hours, in a large shatterproof glass box inside an interrogation room. The blank-walled space lacked the classic desk, chair and mirrored window décor that characterized most police interview rooms. Instead, there was just the cube. His arms were restrained by a yellow straitjacket that fastened in front and his quik-ports were wired to an echo box in the ceiling, where a camera-sensor pod was also mounted. His ankles were shackled to each other and those were connected to a zeta-cable that ran from his receptor port to an encryption box mounted on the floor. There was a heavy lock around his neck, one of his eyeballs was bloody, and his feet were bare on the grid floor, which pressed painfully into his soles. Bio-monitors tracked his skin conductivity, pupil dilation, blush response and a hundred other scan vectors, seeking signs of deception—but for the moment, all he appeared to be was terrified and confused.

The woman who had battered him half to death was pacing circles around him, interrogating him over and over.

"You have the wrong guy," Skinny Man protested, blinking owlishly.

"So tell us who we do have," the Major rejoined.

"My name is Lee Cunningham."

"Where'd you get the weapons?" the Major asked.

"I don't know," Skinny Man said. The Major's gaze flicked to the monitor readings, where a digital needle showed very small tremors over the time-base. She frowned. According to the readout, he thought he was telling the truth.

Still, she pressed on. "Who loaded them onto the truck?"

"I don't know anything about weapons, all right?" Skinny Man exclaimed. "I told you. I was pickin' up my daughter. She takes violin lessons."

"What's her name?"

Skinny Man was exhausted and nervous. It showed in his breathing.

The Major held up a holographic portrait of Skinny Man and showed it to him. "Is this her?"

"Yeah." The suspect couldn't even recognize himself, but the most alarming thing was that he thought he was looking at a child. "Isn't she a little angel?" He beamed at the photo, as if it really did show a little girl he adored.

The Major scanned his face for any sign of mockery. "This is your daughter?" the Major persisted.

"Right," Skinny Man agreed.

Observing, Togusa drew in a whistling breath of incredulity. The poor guy had lost all connection to reality and didn't know it.

"Do you have kids?" Skinny Man asked the

Major, trying to find common ground.

The Major put the holo-portrait away and began circling again. "Where do you live?"

"I can't remember," Skinny Man confessed. "I— I think, I— I think it's a tall place." He looked to her for confirmation, stammering in his growing misery. "Is, is it a tall building? It's a tall place, right?"

The Major skipped over that and went for the throat. "You don't have a child." Skinny Man stared at her in shock. "You don't have a wife," the Major continued. "You live alone. It's just you."

"What?" Skinny Man was devastated. "No."

"We've been to your apartment. There's nobody there."

"No!" Skinny Man shouted, refusing to believe it. Tears prickled at the corner of his eyes as a terrible sorrow welled up inside him.

"You've lived there for ten years by yourself," the Major said.

He was weeping now, shaking his head, denying the Major's words. "No!"

Whatever was going on here, the Major was determined to find out. "So you're just lying."

"*I'm not lying!*" the man howled. He was distraught. "I didn't kill anyone. Why do you keep doin' this to me?"

It was clear that for now, at least, she wouldn't get anything more from him. "Holo cube disconnect," the Major commanded, and her solid-looking holographic image inside the cube disintegrated like falling sand. At a distance from the cube, the Major watched from where she'd been physically the entire time, observing the interrogation with Batou, Ladriya and Togusa.

"Please!" Skinny Man begged, as though he thought the Major was still there with him. "I didn't do anything. Why do you keep saying this to me?"

Ladriya turned to Tagusa for an explanation. "I don't understand. How can he not know?"

Within the cube, Skinny Man kept on sobbing. "Why am I here?"

Togusa sighed. "The hack must have created a vacuum. Kuze has wiped his memory and somehow installed a new reality."

Batou sounded philosophical. "At least he got to believe he had a kid. What's the difference, huh?"

Abruptly, Skinny Man stopped sobbing. His expression became calm and purposeful. The Major noticed, but Batou did not, and expounded on his theory. "Fantasy, reality. Dreams, memories. It's all the same. Just noise."

The Major stood directly outside the cube. Such a monumental falsehood from a man like this suspect, an ordinary working-class citizen with absolutely no training in counter-interrogation techniques, should have blown up as a massive peak on the polygraph. Unless he was a sociopath, there was a far more disturbing possibility at work.

The prisoner walked up to the glass separating them and stared out at her with an unreadable expression, but this was not the same person who had been hysterical with grief and confusion moments ago. His body language was much more controlled. Although this was a new guise, the Major recognized Kuze peering out through the man's eyes. "It's him," she told the team. "He's in there."

Togusa frowned. "This cube is secure. He can't be, Major."

Ladriya looked at the readout. The waveform display had changed from a human-nominal series of tiny peaks and troughs to a completely flat line. There were no tremors at all, not even a hint of displacement. "Lie detector," she realized. The suspect was connected to the polygraph, which was theoretically impregnable, but Kuze had already proved he could get past any firewall. "He must've hacked in that way. We should uplink to the machine, trace the code, get a lock on his location."

"Do it," Togusa urged. Then he saw that the Major was heading for the entrance to the cube. It was one thing for her to put a projection of herself in the cube with the suspect, quite another for her to actually enter it. "Don't go in there. It's too dangerous!"

Aramaki, who had been seated in the corner, silently observing, called out. His face was a mask of grave concern. "Major."

The Major turned to her commander.

"We don't know what else he's capable of," Aramaki cautioned her.

The Major indicated that she understood the warning, and opened the entrance panel in the cube, going inside for the first time to stand face to face with the prisoner. The prisoner studied her with a kind of cold, alien curiosity. The panel closed.

Outside the cube, Ladriya began connecting an echo box to the polygraph, tracing the extra code.

"Signal's unstable," Togusa fretted. "Can you get a lock on it?"

Ladriya was working as fast as she could, but the telemetry wasn't cooperating. "I'm sorry."

"We gotta move fast," Togusa said, just as though Ladriya didn't know this already. "We're losing it."

Ladriya made some adjustments to the echo box, then sighed in relief. "Connecting."

"Who are you?" the Major asked the prisoner.

When the man spoke, it was with Kuze's electronic voice. "Come here."

The Major took a step closer to him.

"I am shy," he softly inhaled. "I'm not beautiful like you."

The Major tried not to be disconcerted. Compliments on her appearance were the last thing she'd expected to hear during the interrogation. "Tell me who you are."

"I have been born more than once," Kuze said through the hacked man's mouth. "So I have more than one name."

"I'll find you," the Major vowed.

"Not yet." Kuze's tone was gentle, but not pleasant. "I'm not done."

Outside the cube, Togusa spoke up. "The machine is tracing his location." He turned to Batou. "We got a fix."

The Major heard, and so did Kuze, who immediately relinquished control of his bio-puppet. She saw the strange shift and change pass over the prisoner's face once again. He looked up at her with watery, panic-stricken eyes, then started trembling and weeping. "I need to see her. Please."

The Major turned away. There was nothing she could do for him. Somehow, seeing him sob for a daughter he'd never had was just about unbearable. She opened the panel and exited the cube.

Behind her, the man continued to beg, whimpering, "No, please. I know... where..."

"We got him," Batou told the Major.

The cube panel shut with a click. Skinny Man leapt up into the air, pulling his legs up underneath him. The cable connecting him to the polygraph was attached to the cube ceiling. His action turned the cable into a noose, snapping his neck. The bio-detectors buzzed with the steady whine of brain and heart flatlining together as he died.

The Major and Batou stared at the dead man through the glass. It had happened so fast, in a single instant, and it had been too late to do anything. Batou exhaled grimly. "Let's go."

7

CITY OF DOLLS

The city's vast urban sprawl clustered along the coastline like some sort of gigantic fungal colony. It spread south toward the lower districts where the habitat blocks rose high, and north into an industrial zone filled with machine-managed factory complexes that worked ceaselessly, many of them operating without human intervention of any kind.

On the sparsely populated edges of the industrial zone, where the police were less inclined to patrol, there existed a ribbon of shanty town sub-districts. Built from reclaimed materials, in the husks of basic habitat blocks for long-gone workers whose jobs had been replaced by synthetics, the shanties were home to criminal elements. They were a place for the displaced and the lost who had slipped through the cracks of the city's society. For now, the edge-town existed in an uneasy truce with the rest of the city.

The government looked the other way as long as the criminals running the place kept it under some kind of control. The yakuza clans held sway there and, in their own way, they managed the shanties as carefully as City Hall did the corporate districts, the harbor zone and the wealthy upper habitats.

Long shadows fell around the garbage-littered street, cast by massive warehouses and manufacturing towers. The tallest was a cylindrical construct of old and cracked concrete, another of the derelict habitats that had been built to house now obsolete human workers.

Togusa took the Section Nine jeepney's wheel. The rest of the team piled into the back, sitting across from each other on the two rough benches on either side. The roads were uneven here, and every now and then someone would lose their grip and bounce, coming down hard.

Even in the darkness, there were signs of life in the industrial fringe. Shipping and crime were both all-hours businesses, after all. But traffic was relatively light on the streets, and soon enough the jeepney was in sight of the warehouse that Kuze had chosen as his base. As hideouts went, it was perfect. There was nothing to distinguish it from a few hundred other buildings in the vicinity.

In the back of the jeepney, Batou ushered orders around the wad of gum in his mouth. "Weapons up."

The agents all raised their guns in compliance.

"Go," Batou said, still chewing.

"On me," the Major directed. She opened the jeepney's back door, and the others filed out behind her.

It was really too bad they had to make such noise on entering, but there was no other way through. Ladriya used adhesive pads to apply C-4 explosive charges to the thick locked door. Everyone stood back as the charges chain-detonated each other in a fiery but contained blast that obliterated the door.

Astonishingly, nobody inside seemed to have heard. A glance down the corridor showed no one responding to the blast, ready to protect yakuza turf. There were no guards on the roof, and no telltale muzzles poking out of interior doorways or at the edges of corners.

The Section Nine agents moved quietly, with all the practiced stealth they could muster, through the warehouse's maze of dark hallways. A fine mist of rain came down steadily inside the building, making the air cold and the floor slippery. The Major gestured for them to halt when they heard distant voices.

A moment of listening to what was being said made it clear that the voices belonged to the kitchen staff. If the workers had any idea that a terrorist was somewhere in the building, they gave no indication of it. Then again, since they worked in a yakuza establishment, maybe such things didn't bother them.

The Section Nine unit continued on their path, unnoticed by the people in the rooms off the hallway.

Different groups of yakuza were scattered about. In one room, several gangsters sat in a circle, wearing nothing but loincloths, all of them watching porn through their virtual reality headsets and moaning in appreciation.

In another room, a woman drilled a quik-port into the neck of a man who was stripped and powdered white like a Butoh dancer. He grunted in discomfort and she blew on his neck to help the port dry.

When they came to a closed door, Batou nodded to Borma, who kicked it in on his first try. Batou charged at the yakuza men inside. They'd been sitting around a table, eating noodles. One man leapt to his feet and went at Batou barehanded. Batou kicked him back down and then shot him for good measure.

The kitchen workers heard the commotion and the gunshot and started shrieking in panic.

Ladriya and Borma, guns at the ready, ran into the room with the VR-watching yakuza. The men were distracted, but not so much that they didn't see the weapons pointed at them. Caught in a tangle of instincts for fight, flight and lust, they barely had time to remember exactly where they'd stashed their own guns, much less reach for them. Ladriya ordered them, "Stay down!" They did. At least two of them made noises in response to their porn viewing that tempted Ladriya to shoot them on grounds of sheer disgust.

In the dining room, Batou advanced on another yakuza soldier, who looked as though he was seriously considering continuing to ingest his noodles rather than bother with the intrusion, giving Batou a hard stare. Then he went for a gun at his waistband and Batou kicked the table into the man's midsection. Before the hoodlum could retaliate Batou put two bullets in him.

The kitchen staff proved difficult. Some of them cowered under the furniture, but others were loyal to the yakuza they served, coming at Major, Ishikawa, and Saito with knives and cleavers. The Section Nine operatives successfully shot all their assailants, emboldened kitchen staff and yakuza soldiers alike.

The tattooed woman who had installed the quik-port ran in from the other room, brandishing her drill threateningly at Ishikawa.

"Put it down!" Ishikawa yelled at her.

The Major spotted another yakuza pulling a pin out of a grenade. She shot him before he could throw it. The dying man fell into a pile of white powder, the grenade dropping from his hand.

Batou saw the grenade rolling just as he entered the kitchen, Tagusa right beside him. "Grenade!" he screamed.

Ishikawa managed to duck as the weapon exploded, blowing white powder all over everyone and everything. The kitchen looked like it had been hit by a blizzard, but no one in Section Nine was injured.

The Major, satisfied her people could take care of themselves, left the kitchen. She advanced through a hallway where more loincloth-wearing yakuza were having white powder applied to their torsos and limbs.

Batou hadn't registered the open cage along the wall. It wasn't until the man squatting inside the cage grabbed him from behind that the agent regretted not paying more attention sooner. Now Batou grappled with the yakuza, trying to free his gun hand.

In another part of the kitchen, the yakuza woman had given up on using her drill for its original purpose and was attempting to club Ishikawa with it. She didn't look round as Batou shot another man, but traded blows with Ishikawa until he was able to knock her out.

The Major continued deeper into the warehouse, making her way through a labyrinth of deserted underground corridors. In one room, dead and dying men hung suspended from the ceiling in enormous plastic disposal bags. Those still living whimpered, but did not attempt to free themselves. The Major could see they were too far gone to help and besides, they were yakuza. She did not want to turn them loose.

In another room, this one much larger, dozens of white-powdered, shaven-headed men in monks' robes sat in two concentric circles, every single one with the same vacant expression on his face. Each man had a high-speed zeta-cable jacked into his receptor ports, and the thick wires coiled away into fat bunches that rose together to form a dome of strands that ran into the ceiling, tap roots for heavy traffic junction boxes and server arrays.

The Major took a deep breath and went inside. In the air all around her were snatches of overlapping, garbled Internet conversations, almost as unsettling as the seated men who were here physically but not mentally. Or were they conscious in any way? The Major peered at them, curious. Then realization came.

"*Major!*" Batou called to her over the mind-comm. "*Come in.*"

"*I know why we couldn't find him,*" she told Batou over the comm. "*He's using human minds to create a network of his own.*" These men were data hosts who had been kidnapped, blackmailed or bribed by Kuze so that their brains could be used as Internet servers. Kuze was routing his code through them to cover his tracks. Which meant that they connected to him.

"*We're coming to your position,*" Batou told her.

On some level, the Major knew that she ought to stay where she was and wait for back up, but every fiber of her body was tense with the need to push on and find Kuze. She needed to confront him, to look him in the eyes for real this time. Nothing else would be enough. She kept walking, her attention on the passageway ahead. For a moment, she sensed something in her peripheral vision, but when she turned to look, all she saw was more gray, wet hallway.

She passed another room full of bagged yakuza victims. She kept going.

What stopped the Major in her tracks was another glitch. The burning pagoda was in front of her again.

This time, a teenage Japanese girl was being dragged out of it by the New Port City police. A teenage boy, also Japanese, was trying to pull the girl away from her captors. The girl was screaming in distress. "Hideo!" she shouted, and the Major understood this must be the boy's name. Then the glitch disappeared.

Without warning, a yakuza gangbanger burst out of the darkness and stabbed a brutal-looking stun baton at the Major's chest. It was a close cousin to the device No Pupils had tortured her with back at the Sound Business nightclub. Thousands of volts arced between the steel tines at its tip, threatening pain and feedback damage through her mech nerves if it made contact.

But this time she was ready. As if a switch had flipped inside her head, the Major was instantly in attack mode. Instead of retreating, or even going for her pistol, she launched herself at the man.

Her limbs became a blur of kicks and punches, parrying his attacks one after another as she drove him backward. The snarling yakuza found a lucky opening and managed to land a swift, glancing blow with the stun baton, but she deflected it before the weapon could release a full charge into her. They fought viciously in the tightly enclosed space, pirouetting around one another in an obscene, savage waltz. The Major sent quick, hard chopping impacts into his chest, snapping his ribs where each blow landed.

The thug reacted, crying out in agony, and she

smashed him across the throat with a cobra-strike punch. He fell to the floor, no longer a threat to her— but he had not been alone. She dropped a second assailant, but then another heavily tattooed yakuza enforcer was right there, a taser in his fist. He didn't wait for her to react, just jammed the business end of the device into her quik-port.

Losing control of her movements, the Major sank to the floor. The voltage flooded through her and there was nothing she could do as the yakuza guard jabbed the prod at her ports repeatedly, electrocuting her again and again. The Major had a strong tolerance for electricity but when more men joined in with their own weapons, five hundred thousand volts of screaming energy shot through her cybernetic body. The Major's last sensory input was the smell of the cheap tobacco on the man's breath.

Then darkness came and took her.

8

PROJECT 2571

This time, when the Major awoke, the jarring shift in place and time felt almost *human*.

There was no instantaneous transition from the non-state of inaction to the full awareness of being present. The wetware of her organic brain struggled to process the events, and slowly her senses returned to her.

She was floating above a dirty concrete floor. At first she thought that, impossibly, gravity had ceased to function around her. Then she became aware of her body's own weight, all of it concentrated around her neck and the steel column of her artificial spine. There was a vise-like device holding her head in place, connected at her temples, and her feet did not reach the ground.

Odd collisions of noise and ambient sound washed back and forth through her neural processors until at length they began to separate out into distinct nodes. Somewhere off to her right, water dripped in a steady metronome-tick rhythm. Behind her, an electric generator was humming softly, providing power to the faint lights arrayed up above.

Her processors filtered out more sounds. Mechanical noises nearby, the soft irregular click of manipulators and the whisper of motion.

"Hello?" She tried to reach out with her mind-comms link, but the system was dead and everything she did to try to reactivate it only emphasized her powerlessness. The same was true of her legs and her arms, dangling inert and useless. This was not the result of the stun-shock that had knocked her offline. Someone had activated a neural shunt, bypassing the command pathways from her brain case to the rest of her central operating functions. She could open her eyes, she could speak, move her head a little. But nothing else. Her captor had been very thorough.

She was hanging from the ceiling by cables jacked into the ports on her neck. The shunt that digitally paralyzed her from the neck down was in there, working its control over her body. With effort, the Major shifted her gaze and took in the chamber around her fully for the first time. Her internal chronometer showed that twenty minutes had elapsed since the fight in the junction room. She was somewhere else now, in what looked like an old survival bunker from the chaos of the Third War. This was the underground bunker from her visions of Kuze.

And here, really present and not a hologram, was the man still covered by his hooded robe.

Despite her vulnerable position, when the Major spoke, it was a demand. "Tell me who you are."

The man's reply came with computer stutters and glitches, as well as the occasional electronic buzz. For all his technological brilliance, this was something he could not fix, or else did not wish to. "I am that which you seek to destroy." His voice echoed slightly after he finished speaking. "In this life my name is... Kuze."

The Major's every instinct was to fight against the cables holding her, but she couldn't move. "What are you doing to me?"

"I have c-connected you... to a network of my own creation," Kuze told her. "Wh-wh-when I am finished in this world... my ghost can survive there and re-regenerate." He walked with a rolling limp, slightly unbalanced, but it did not lessen his powerful presence.

Kuze had proved beyond doubt that he had no hesitation about killing people, scientists, law enforcement and civilians alike. Why had he taken the Major prisoner instead of taking her life? "What do you want from me?" she asked.

"I became... fascinated with you." And then Kuze removed his cloak and revealed himself. The Major met his gaze.

Intact and complete, he would have been quite

handsome. But the visage beneath the hood was distorted, as if shown through a cracked lens. He had the face of a Caucasian man, or at least part of a face. Some of it was bare bioroid skull. He looked to be about the Major's age, and it appeared that he had been assembled as she had been. But in his case, many of the parts fit poorly and much of the shielding was absent, leaving his inner robotic workings exposed. Tech mesh covered his right side and his chest was open in the middle, revealing cyber-organs beneath. His synthetic ribcage was clearly visible from the back, open to the elements, naked machine skeleton and titanium spine. The left side of his faceplate was metal, with no epidermis, and the skin on the right side of his face was scarred. The fingers of his right hand were bare metal, but the back of the hand had skin tattooed with the image of a woman's eye. He had another tattoo on his left shoulder.

There was a peculiar androgynous beauty to him, a strange sort of fragility that masked what the Major knew of his deadly nature. His eyes were green, and looked as though whoever had crafted them had made them as much or more to simulate pure human emotion than as receptors for his cyber upgrades.

The Major knew they were only implants, but still she was unsettled by their expression. What was it... hunger? Rage? Surely not... affection?

He was standing before her, real and within her grasp, if only her hands could reach and subdue him.

Kuze continued with his explanation, the electronic buzz making the words stutter. "Reading your, your-your-your code while you were inside that geisha. Like nothing I had... felt before and yet so... familiar. We are the same."

The Major's body was numb, but she felt searing fury at the comparison. She kept her voice level, knowing that a show of temper would only put her at more of a disadvantage. "We are not the same. You kill innocent people."

"Innocent, is that, th-th-that what you call them?" Through all the glitching and buzzing, Kuze still sounded wry. "I am as they... made me."

The Major suddenly experienced a sinking sense of doubt, hoping she was wrong. "Who made you?"

He cocked his head, a wry smile playing over mismatched lips. "What have they told you? That you were the first? The first cerebral s-salvage?" The green eye implants shone with what appeared to be strong emotion and his voice grew rueful. "You were born of-of-of lessons they took from-from my failure."

The Major did not want to believe what he was implying. "What are you talking about?"

For all the distortion in his voice, Kuze's bitterness was clear. "I was conscious while they dismembered my body and discarded me... like garbage."

She said nothing. She could not. He was saying that he was an earlier, failed prototype of the experimental process that had resulted in her new life. If it was the same process, it was the same scientists. Hanka scientists. He was saying that they had dismantled him after they determined that he was not a viable prototype. And that they—that Genevieve Ouelet—had been lying to the Major all along. It wasn't possible.

"I... was lying on a table," Kuze went on, "listening to doctors talk about how my-my mind had not meshed with the shell that they had... built." A shade of anger crept into his voice. "How Project 2571... had failed... and they had to move on... to you."

The electrocution by his minions, the paralysis, these had been violation enough, but he was not finished. Kuze placed his fingers upon a set of contact points hidden beneath the synthetic flesh of the Major's face and applied careful pressure. There was a wet click in her jaw and the seams of her cheek plating bubbled to the surface. He removed the left side of her faceplate, leaving the synthetic skull open from forehead to upper lip, exposing the complex circuitry, artificial musculature and alloy bones beneath that comprised the structure of her face.

The Major gasped, not because it hurt—she could not feel it at all—but because it was both so invasive and so intimate. And because Kuze looked neither disgusted nor clinical, the two emotions she'd seen in those few humans who'd seen inside her shell. What he saw inside her seemed to leave him... entranced.

"What a beauty you are," Kuze said to the Major.

He brought the disconnected cheek plate close to his face, as if it was a delicate flower and he wanted to bask in the scent. "They have improved us... so much... since they made me." He paused. "They thought that we would be a part of their evolution, but... they have created us... to evolve alone..."

He reattached the section of the Major's faceplate that he'd been holding. It snapped back into place easily, its joins undetectable. "...beyond them," Kuze concluded.

So Kuze really thought he and the Major were some kind of new breed, superior to humans? "Evolution," she taunted him, "that's what you call killing everyone who made you?"

Kuze sounded frustrated. "You-you're not... listening to me."

The Major felt that she'd listened quite enough. "You're a murderer."

"They-they-they tried to kill me first." The buzzing of his artificially generated voice grew louder. "It is... self-defense." He slapped his own chest, indignant. "Defense of self!" He lowered his voice. "More will die... until they tell me what they took!" Enraged and despondent, he slapped his own head.

"I won't let that happen." The Major knew that Kuze could destroy her if he kept her paralyzed, but in his belief that they were connected he seemed unwilling to do so.

Kuze backed up this theory by making a sound

of inarticulate anger, then running up and putting his face right up against the Major's, yet making no move to harm her. "You want to kill me?" He studied her eyes for a reaction. "Like everyone else." He looked resigned. "Do it then."

And then Kuze astonished the Major by pressing his head against her chest and embracing her. "Do what you were programmed to do," he murmured, a taunt of his own, implying that she had no free will, only thoughts that had been implanted in her mind.

Then he freed her, reaching up to her neck to disengage the neural shunt.

At once, all the cables let go of her. No longer suspended above the floor, the Major fell, gasping and shaken, slumping onto Kuze's shoulder. Her body's active cyber-systems suddenly flooded back into her control and it was like a hot wave engulfing her.

He gently lowered her to the ground. The Major immediately grabbed the pistol from his belt, then punched him clear across the room and fired at him repeatedly.

Kuze staggered to a stop. The gunshots had barely fazed him. The Major noticed something, stopped her attack, and approached him. Her attention was caught so completely that she was no longer worried what the killer might do next. "What is that?" she asked.

On his chest, Kuze bore a large blue-black tattoo of something the Major could not forget: rendered in delicate strokes, the pagoda from her visions.

She was so distressed that she slapped at the tattoo, as though the image on Kuze's body had somehow caused the images in her mind. "*What is that?*"

"I c-can't remember," Kuze said, plaintive. "B-but I am haunted by it. Do you see it?"

She was staggered. Kuze saw the same glitches that she did. She could accept that there was something about the brain implantation process that caused glitches, but why the hell should it cause two different subjects to see exactly the same thing? What had happened to both of them?

Elsewhere in the warehouse, Batou and Togusa were chasing the Major's signal as quickly as they could. It had been inactive for some while, but now it was on again and they intended to speed to her side—while fighting their way through the yakuza guards that kept springing into their path. Despite the fact that the Section Nine agents were better armed, better trained and a lot better prepared than their enemies, Batou was starting to have some concerns about how much ammo they had left.

And yet more yakuza poured into the hallway. "Togusa!" Batou yelled. Togusa sprang to the side to kick down a closed door, while Batou lay down a spray of covering fire for him, mowing down the men trying to kill them both.

The Major had stopped fighting Kuze and was listening to what he had to tell her. It was horrible, it turned her world upside down, but there was too much proof he was telling the truth.

"Don't... take the medication... that they give you," he warned her. "They use it to suppress your memories. Your shell belongs to them, but not your ghost. Your ghost is yours. Remember that, and maybe you... can remember it all."

He might have said more, but a grenade blast tore one of the doors off its hinges. Batou and Togusa sprinted in through the roiling dust. Batou at once levelled his gun at Kuze. "Get away from her!" Batou shouted. "Get down on the ground... now!"

Kuze pulled two Uzis, firing them simultaneously at Batou and Togusa until the weapons clicked on empty. The two agents ducked for cover and returned fire, but no one was struck in the exchange. Kuze dropped the machine guns, turned and ran, vanishing into the surrounding darkness. Somewhere down the hall, a door slammed.

"Major!" Batou shouted.

He was relieved to see that she appeared unharmed—but she was staring at him with distrust. In disbelief, Batou watched as the Major turned and fled through the doorway. "Major!" he shouted again. He got no answer.

9

STAND ALONE

The residential tower was a city within the city, a self-contained vertical ark that could accommodate all the needs of any of its well-heeled occupants without them ever having to leave the confines of the building. Only Hanka's best and brightest resided here, where each apartment was a penthouse in itself, an isolated retreat from the rest of the city's tumult far below.

From the outside, the hundred-story condominium was aesthetically pleasing. The windows in all of its many apartments were round rather than square, with the philosophy that the inhabitants could look outside and see a world that was, for them, literally globe-shaped. The theory was that this provided perspective, a calming start to the day and end to the night: this was where you were in the place of things.

The interior echoed the exterior, walls painted neutral pinkish beige, with rounded archways instead of rectangular doorways. The archways led from the living room to several smaller spaces barely larger than alcoves, each one two steps up from the main floor, with walls that curved to a rounded ceiling.

Genevieve Ouelet had made one of these smaller spaces her bedroom. The whole apartment was spartan, with no furniture save for bathroom fixtures and the yellow-tiled block for viewing holo data in the center of the living room. Ouelet didn't even have a bed. She lay sleeping on a thin mattress covered with a nest of blankets on the bedroom floor, exhausted from the day's horrendous events. Even the ceiling light overhead did not wake her.

The Major stood quietly over the sleeping doctor. She had shown her Section Nine identification to the doorman, so he was obliged to let her inside. The Major had told the doorman that Dr. Ouelet was expecting her. Perhaps that was even true. She had never been here before. Something had always made it seem improper for her to cross the boundary between Ouelet's working world in the labs and the office at Hanka, and the doctor's personal world here in the tower.

Ouelet would have slept through until morning, but she sensed something amiss. The perception pierced her dream state, enough to wake her. For an instant, Ouelet thought the shadow falling across her was a remnant of her dream. Then she saw it really was the Major, understood that she was awake, and gasped.

"Oh, Mira." Ouelet sighed in relief. "Oh, my God, you're safe!" She expected a friendly response and waited. When the Major didn't speak, Ouelet filled in the silence. "You've been gone for hours!" She swallowed. "And no one knew where you were."

The Major said nothing. She just kept up her level stare, straight into Ouelet's eyes.

"What?" Ouelet was pleading now. "You're scaring me."

When the Major stepped forward, Ouelet instinctively retreated, scrambling backward on hands and bent knees until she was in the bottom of the wall's curve. This was totally unlike Mira. "Calm down," the doctor instructed, trying to contain her fear.

The Major finally spoke, and her tone was calm enough. It was her words that frightened Ouelet. "How many were there before me?"

Ouelet contemplated her options and decided there was no point in trying to deflect the question. The Major clearly knew there had been experimental prototypes before her, robots implanted with human brains. She tried to answer in a way that would blunt the Major's anger. "The intricacies of shelling your mind, it had never been done before. It was inevitable there would be failures."

"How many?"

"Dozens," Ouelet conceded.

The Major wanted the exact number. "How many?" she repeated.

"Ninety-eight unsuccessful attempts before you."
The enormity of the admission fell between them.
Ouelet's regret appeared genuine, but the Major
didn't care.

The Major's head moved up and down, less a nod
than an attempt to contain her rising outrage. "You
killed ninety-eight innocent people."

"No, I di—" Ouelet stammered over her protest
and tried again, "didn't kill anyone. You wouldn't
be here. You wouldn't exist if it... if it weren't for
those experiments."

"'Experiments'?" Now the Major was the one
backing away. She felt an urgent need to get away
from this woman, this lying, manipulative hypocrite
who had positioned herself as a surrogate mother. "Is
that what I am to you?"

"No!" Ouelet protested.

But the Major turned and walked out of the
bedroom.

Ouelet scrambled to her feet and rushed into the
living room after her, so quickly that the bottom of her
lightweight night-robe lifted and floated behind her as
she ran. "No, Mira!" The Major wouldn't meet her
gaze, but stared pensively into the middle distance.

Ouelet began anew with her explanation.
"Sacrifices were made."

"Where did the bodies come from?" the Major
wanted to know. "Where did I come from?" She
turned to Ouelet and advanced again.

"Mr. Cutter brought them to us," Ouelet said. Her tone was defensive. Then it became ashamed. "I didn't ask questions."

The Major no longer knew whether to be angry or despairing or just numb to the core. Every fact she had known about herself was falling away and breaking. "The harbor! My parents. The way they died. Did that happen?" The memories of the refugee boat, of people drowning in the harbor, still seemed real, but they felt different from the memories of the pagoda and even the cat, the memories in the glitches.

Ouelet took her time before she finally confessed, her eyes downcast. "No. We gave you false memories. Cutter wanted to motivate you. To fight terrorists. I didn't approve. It was cruel, but my work, it was important, and you were born. You were *so* beautiful." Ouelet reached out a hand to touch her splendid creation, the child that had been birthed by her work, but the Major grabbed her hand to stop her.

She had been lied to by Ouelet: about her memories, her parents, the reason that she existed. The Major was so livid she could barely get the words out. "Nothing I have is real." Before she could lie to her once more, the Major said flatly, "I found him."

Ouelet knew the Major was talking about Kuze. Her face reflected her dismay. "I told you to be careful."

"You knew where he was the whole time," the Major accused. "You built him."

Ouelet desperately wanted Mira to understand what

had happened with Kuze. "He had a violent, unstable mind. The cerebral connections wouldn't hold!"

The Major began walking to the door. Ouelet continued, pleading her case to Mira's back. "I tried to save him!"

This might have been Ouelet's cruelest lie yet. "No," the Major said. "You left him to die." She went out through the apartment door. Ouelet's lip trembled as she lowered her head in despair, but the Major never turned back.

A pair of hycops, helicopter drones with airplane-style wings, soared above New Port City, training red searchlights on the ground below as they conducted radar scans of every floor of every building.

In the streets below, Batou monitored the scans as he maneuvered his car through the traffic. "*Nothing on Kuze yet, sir,*" he reported to Aramaki over the mind-comm. "*Checking upper zones next.*" He was more concerned with the answer to his own question. "*Is there any word on Major?*"

Aramaki's voice betrayed nothing. "*She's gone. Off-grid. Silent.*"

So the Major had cut herself off from all communications and computer networks, and was thus untraceable. Unless you knew her as a person. As Batou did. "*Copy that, sir. I know where to find her.*"

* * *

At the bottom of New Port City Harbor, the water was dark and cold, a world separate from the one above. In the depths of the night-dark sea, there was only the faint shimmer of shifting tides, and scant light trickling in from far above. The Major hung in blue-black water, slowly descending as gravity pulled her down. As she went deeper, the sounds of the distant city began to fade, gradually to be replaced by a thick, all-encompassing silence. Her eyes opened as she sank.

Despite the pollution that had killed a lot of life here, hardy thick kelp stretched up from the bottom and large, bioluminescent white jellyfish were all around. Unlike humans, the jellyfish were not taken in by the Major's exterior. They sensed that she was mainly inorganic matter, which made her neither prey nor threat. When they brushed against her, their trailing poisonous tentacles did not sting.

The Major would not have cared if they had. This was her chosen place of contemplation, where she could think without distraction or disturbance. There were no lies here, no deceptions, no contradictions, only silence that had been much the same since the Earth had cooled eons ago. There was no data here, either, nothing that could have made the Major what she was. It was a world in which Ouelet, and Hanka, and all the rest had no place. Finally, she reached the muddy floor of the channel and let her body settle to the ground, causing clouds of disturbed sand to billow about her.

Her dark hair floated around her head in small tendrils, making her look a bit like some exotic marine creature, as she stood upright on the harbor floor, reaching inside herself for some fraction of serenity. Down here, she needed no apparatus to breathe. Down here, she did not need to pretend she was a normal human being.

Here and here alone, in the nothingness—at least for a time—she could be herself.

The Major recognized the shadow of a watercraft above her. She wore a wetsuit with diver's flippers, and now she used them to paddle and push as she ascended. Dawn had not come yet. She surfaced next to the small boat bobbing in the harbor's mild currents. Far off on shore, a dull rainbow glow came from the city's lights and holograms, reflecting in the low waves. White lanterns on the boat's sides provided more distinct illumination.

At one time, the little old-fashioned craft had been a tugboat. Batou had bought it on a whim, intending to take it out on fishing trips, but the choppy waters around the bay and the baseline toxicity in the local marine life disabused him of that idea. He had a line over the side nevertheless, but he mainly used the boat for drinking and generally getting away from people. From here, it seemed like the shore was one massive urban sprawl extending as far as the eye could see.

An endless city, from horizon to horizon. Like the Major, he felt the need to leave it behind on occasion.

He saw her head emerge from the ink-black depths of the channel. She glared, looking annoyed to see him. He waited on the wooden deck while the Major pulled herself in over the side and landed gracefully on her feet. Her epidermis reacted to the cold and she shivered. "I didn't ask you to come here," she said.

"You never ask," Batou replied. "But I always do." There was no resentment in his words. He tossed her a towel, sat down next to a fishing pole and took a swig of beer from a can.

"Did they send you to bring me in?" the Major pressed.

Batou took another swallow of beer. "I'm just here to fish. Did you see any?"

The Major wasn't having his casual act. "You're a company man, you follow orders, so if they ordered you to kill me…"

Batou was hurt, but he tried to keep his tone light. "Stop saying shit like that. You're gonna piss me off."

He grabbed another can of beer. When he turned to offer it to her, she shook her head, so Batou tossed the beer can back into the cooler.

"What's it like down there?" He'd always wanted to ask her, but somehow never had before.

"It's cold and dark. Just a million miles away. No voices. No data streaming. Just… nothing." She took a breath. "It scares me."

"Then why do you do it?"

The Major did not respond at once. Batou took another swig of beer. Then she answered him. "It feels real."

Batou had something more urgent he wanted to ask, about the Major's unexpected reaction to Kuze. "Why didn't you stop him?"

"I don't know who to trust anymore."

He felt saddened, and a little uneasy. "You trust me, right?" Batou had to ask.

The Major turned and studied him for a moment, then dipped her head in a nod. "Yeah, I do. I just don't like it."

Batou couldn't help grinning. The Major was all business. Any emotion, even trust, was bound to vex her, but that was one of the things he liked about her. Any loyalties she had were hard-won, and true.

The Major stepped into the boat's tiny cabin. It didn't have a door, so she kept her back to Batou as she peeled off the dark blue wetsuit, then toweled herself dry. He turned in the opposite direction to give her privacy. It would be completely improper for him to ever think of the Major in a romantic sense. Even so, Batou was acutely aware of her appearance and the exceptional curves of her female form, and he would be mortified if he ever did anything to alert her to that awareness.

"I need you to take me back," she told him. "There's more I need to find out."

"Sure." Batou swallowed the last of his beer.

Ouelet felt even more miserable than she had before, in part because what had happened during the Major's visit had had time to fully sink in, and in part because there were now two Hanka guards posted in her apartment, watching her every move as she communicated with Cutter over the comm.

Cutter was in his office. His holographic image perfectly conveyed exactly how angry he was. "Dr. Ouelet, what have you told her?"

He was asking both about Project 2571 overall and Kuze specifically. "She knows," Ouelet replied into the comm. There was no point in trying to keep this from Cutter; he'd find out anyway.

"I'm bringing her in," Cutter informed her.

Batou went forward to secure the bow line as the Major leapt off the boat. She reached for the vial of medication she kept with her, no matter where she was. It was time for her morning dose. She had the vial in her hand—and then remembered what Kuze had said about the medication's true purpose. Right now, she was more inclined to believe him than the Hanka doctors. Instead of absorbing the medication via her quik-ports, she threw the full vial into the bay.

She heard a vehicle motor. Hard-earned reflexes

made both the Major and Batou react. They were halfway toward reaching for their sidearms when a Hanka security team poured out of a jeepney. The private soldiers wore black ballistic armor and masks, and were armed with machine guns, which they pointed straight at the Major. She might have been able to take all of them on by herself. Had this been part of a mission, she certainly would have tried. But Batou would be caught in the crossfire, and if by some miracle he survived that, he'd be arrested for trying to help her.

The team leader spoke aloud into his comm. "Hanka Security to headquarters. We have the Major."

10

DISCONNECT

Once more at Hanka Robotics, literally the last place she wanted to revisit, the Major was strapped to a gurney, being wheeled down a corridor by a red-gowned surgical team. She could do nothing except wonder if this would be like the last time it happened, when she'd been put under and awakened to a set of new, false memories.

Then she glitched. The two teenagers she'd seen in her vision of the burning pagoda were here, in a Hanka surgical prep room. Both of them were restrained at the waist, and tied down to separate gurneys. They reached for each other, hands just touching, but the contact was short-lived as the doctors pulled them apart.

"Motoko!" Hideo cried out.

The girl sobbed. She and Hideo had been so happy, and then—why had they been taken? Why were they here? The Major was only observing the glitch, but she knew what was in Motoko's soul.

"Motoko!" Hideo cried again. He reached for her.

She tried to reach for him. "Hideo!" She was disconsolate.

"Let's go," a male doctor said. Hideo's thrashing, grasping arm was pulled back. The glitch ended. The Major didn't feel as sure of Hideo's emotions as she had Motoko's, but she still empathized with how the young man in her vision had felt. She was alone in Ouelet's operating room for the moment, but at least she was sitting up in the exam chair rather than lying flat. The Major was sedated, woozy from the drugs and restrained by a device clamped around the upper portion of her skull. She tried to crane her neck for a look through the observation window into Ouelet's office, but the angle was wrong, and besides, the apparatus around her head made it difficult to bend her neck. The sedatives made her feel as though her body and limbs had been filled with cement.

Snatching a few hours of troubled, turbulent sleep had not helped Genevieve Ouelet to salve her conscience, so she turned back to the single thing that could give her peace—the work.

Returning to her lab in the pre-dawn hours, she had set to processing the analysis of a new neural substrate software model, but even this could not stop her focus from drifting. Each time she closed her eyes, she saw Mira Killian's face, filled with raw hurt and accusation.

Ouelet had been troubled by rumors around the building, talk among the security staff that Mira had been suspended from her duties at Section Nine and was now being considered a flight risk... even a potential *threat*.

She didn't want to believe that. She didn't want to consider that she had been responsible in some way.

The scientist kept replaying their last conversation over and over in her mind, wondering if there was something else she could have said, some way she could have handled things differently so that Mira would not have vanished into the night.

Cutter was watching the Major through the large observation window separating Ouelet's office from the operating room. The doctor entered her workplace and joined the executive by the window.

Cutter noted the small-scale model of Project 2571's unadorned shell on her desk. There was also a humanoid skull and a little vial of yellow medication. Ouelet wasn't one for decoration, so clearly the shell and the skull had deep meaning for her. The medication was no doubt because Ouelet didn't yet understand what was going to happen.

"Why is she sedated?" Ouelet asked.

Cutter gave her a patronizing look. "She's been turned by a terrorist. But you know that already."

Ouelet said nothing. Instead, she sat down at

her desk and looked away.

"You should've called the first time she came to see you," Cutter continued. His tone was acid. "Instead, you gave her information."

Ouelet's temper flared. This *connard* had seriously expected her to betray Mira to him? "What makes you think you have the right to tell me what to do and what—"

Cutter spoke right over her. "2571 took us close." Ouelet know that what he meant was not her definition of success—a perfect meld of human and synthetic—but rather a creation that would be totally loyal to Hanka. "It's time to move on to the next iteration."

The color drained from Ouelet's face, horrified at the implication in Cutter's words. "2571 is not a failure. I'll delete all the data and reprogram her. She won't remember him at all."

But Cutter had made up his mind. "No. No, no, no, no, no. You download all the data on the terrorist, and then I order you to terminate."

Ouelet was stunned. She knew that she had heard Cutter correctly, though she desperately wished that she hadn't. She felt close to tears. "What?" She felt sick, hollowed out by what Cutter was demanding from her.

"You'll build one that's better," Cutter assured her.

She tried to bargain with him. "I'll delete everything."

Cutter knew as well as Ouelet did that even a

total memory wipe didn't guarantee that rebellion wouldn't form in the subject's brain all over again. "You've deleted before."

Mira was Ouelet's creation. Cutter was overstepping his authority here. "She's mine," the doctor countered.

"No," Cutter said. "She's a contract. With me."

Mira was more than an experiment that had come to fruition; she was a living being. Ouelet would not kill her. As head of Hanka Robotics, Cutter shouldn't want this either. "We succeeded," she told him.

Cutter inhaled angrily, mustering another retort.

"She's more than human," Ouelet continued. "And more than AI. We changed her entire identity. But her ghost survived!"

"Her *ghost* is what failed us," Cutter spat back. "We cannot control her. She's no longer a viable asset."

Cutter took a vial of red liquid from his pocket. Ouelet knew exactly what the substance was. Applied to a quik-port, it would cause all functions to cease, both biological and cybernetic. He placed the vial on Ouelet's desk. "You should be the one to do it."

Ouelet entered the operating room and began working at the computer terminal attached to the Major's head.

The Major held on to a kernel of cold fury at the indignity of her treatment. Her life and her freedom had been removed as cleanly as the flesh of the old, human body she didn't remember, and there was nothing she could do to prevent it. She wondered what Section Nine had been told about her. Had Cutter convinced them that she had been suborned by Kuze, that she was now as much a threat as he was? Were they ready to shoot her on sight? Not Batou, never Batou, but the others... What did Aramaki believe?

Ouelet was behind her, so the Major couldn't make eye contact, but maybe that was just as well. "What are you doing to me?" Her words were slurred from the sedation.

The doctor's voice was soft and reassuring. "I'll run the standard synaptic, upload your data on the raid. Find out exactly what Kuze told you."

"You *know* what he told me," the Major retorted. She might be drugged, but she wasn't so out of it that she wasn't infuriated that Ouelet was still keeping up the pretense that the Major was mistaken. "The truth."

From the office, Cutter observed the interaction through the window. Why was Ouelet prolonging the inevitable? Guilt? Wanting to spend a little more time with her prized specimen before starting over?

Ouelet typed more commands into the computer.

"You're deleting everything, aren't you?" the Major said. She wondered what memories would be implanted this time. The same ones about the terrorist attack in the harbor, or some new scenario? It didn't matter. Whoever she was now would be gone.

"No," Ouelet said.

This time, the Major hoped Ouelet was lying. If not... "Make it so I don't remember... you."

Ouelet winced, glad that Mira could not see how that struck home. Not that the doctor blamed her patient. Ouelet inserted a small tool into a hidden pin hole socket concealed within the Major's black hair at the back of her head. With a high-pitched click, the tool rotated and the back of the Major's skull opened like a flower, petals of artificial skin and polymer-ceramic skull plates peeling back to expose the dark titanium brain case beneath. Within the case, sheathed in a complex web of molecule-thin connectors, the Major's organic brain was suspended in a bath of processing fluids and support nutrients.

The Major began to recite the rote statement required at the start of every cyber-medical procedure. "My name is Major Mira Killian, and I..." she deviated from what she'd said every other time, "do *not* consent to the deletion of this data."

Ouelet used the manipulator tool to open a second hidden port beneath the brain case, presenting a receptor plug for an intravenous chemical line.

"I do not consent," the Major repeated. "I do not consent."

"We never needed your consent," Ouelet told Mira, sadly. "Yours or anyone's."

So the consent was just a ruse that Hanka used as a form of false reassurance, making their cyber-enhanced subjects compliant and trusting. Even that had been a lie. The Major realized out loud, "You're killing me... aren't you?" Tears welled up in her eyes. It wasn't the prospect of death, but rather that everything she'd known was false. She had trusted Ouelet, having absolute faith that the doctor was saving what was human in her, keeping her human. Instead, she had been taking it away. Now it was going to end, and none of it was true. Perhaps she should be glad it was over.

Ouelet saw the moment unfold in her thoughts before she committed to it. In an odd way, it was like watching a hologram commercial, a three-dimensional image moving through a series of pre-programmed motions over and over. Abstract and unchanging. In its own way, *inevitable*.

Before her, Mira's body lay tense and trembling against the support frame.

Ouelet kept her hands low. She knew that Cutter was observing through the window. She did not want him to see that the vial she inserted into the injector was filled with yellow liquid, not the red he had given her. Ouelet did not speak as she attached the inoculation device to a syringe, then plunged the syringe directly into Mira's brain.

The Major gasped, reacting to the drugs.

Ouelet replaced the portion of skull she had removed and stepped around the side of the operating table, so that her back was to the observation window and Cutter beyond it. Mira could now see her face. She spoke very quietly. "Mira? Can you hear me?"

Keeping her hand below where it could be seen from the other room, Ouelet pressed a button. The restraints unclamped from the Major's skull, leaving her free.

Cutter didn't need to see exactly what Ouelet was doing to realize something was wrong. He turned from the window and moved to the office door.

"Mira, this is your past." Ouelet took something from her pocket and pressed it into the Major's hand. "Your real past. Take it."

The Major looked down at her palm, not yet understanding. Lying there against her flawless artificial skin was an old mechanical key stamped with numbers, attached to a keychain with a fob bearing the inscription *1912 Avalon Apartments*.

She no longer felt drowsy and heavy. Instead, energy was coursing through her body, both its biological and synthetic components. Her limbs were free.

In Ouelet's office, Cutter pressed the button to open the door so that he could go into the operating room. The door remained shut. He began to pound on it. "Guards!"

Ouelet swept the dazed Major's legs off the exam chair and set her upright on her feet. "Come on, *come on*!" Ouelet entreated. "Come on, go!"

Pulling Major along with her, Ouelet ran to the door. Two Hanka guards were standing outside.

Ouelet gasped in dismay. The guards shoved her out of the way, charging at Major.

The Major lashed out with a few strategically placed blows that laid both men out cold on the floor. In the doorway, she turned to look back at Ouelet. The doctor was sitting on the floor, not poised to run or even stand.

"Go," Ouelet said, tears coursing down her face. "Go!"

The Major hesitated a moment longer, then ran alone into the corridor.

"Hey!" a third guard yelled as he charged at her.

The Major swung a truncheon that she'd taken from one of the downed guards in the operating room. The weapon connected solidly with the charging guard, the impact rendering him unconscious.

A female voice spoke over the facility's PA system. "Security alert on Level Twenty-Five."

A door swung open and another guard came running out, gun aimed. He shot at the Major, who threw herself to her knees and used her momentum to slide into the guard's legs, knocking him over.

He groaned in pain as two more guards ran into the corridor. The Major sprang up, using the baton to subdue one of the men as he fired his gun ineffectually. She grabbed the guard's gun hand, struggling to control the weapon.

"Initiating lock-down procedure," the PA system announced.

The Major squeezed the guard's hand, his finger still on the trigger, shooting the second guard coming at them. The Major switched her grip on the guard she was holding and hurled him into the wall.

"Please," the PA system urged, "relocate to your designated safe room."

The Major took a moment to catch her breath and evaluate the situation. She ran back down the corridor and grabbed the guard's gun off the floor.

"Security alert on Level Twenty-Five," the PA system repeated. "Please relocate to your designated safe room. Thank you for your cooperation."

Still trapped in Ouelet's office, Cutter couldn't quite believe what had happened. He knew Ouelet was arrogant, but this was too much. She had proved beyond a doubt that she couldn't be trusted, in her judgments or her actions. He glared at her through the observation window as she got up from the operating room floor and turned to look at him. There was no apology in her face, not that it mattered now. She had put sentiment for 2571 over her professional obligations, over her duty to Hanka, over Cutter's orders. It was unforgivable.

Ouelet's value was really only in what she had brought to the projects. Her research was at Cutter's fingertips and there were many other genius-level IQs at Hanka Robotics that could pick up where she left off—less involved, less sentimental scientists who would relish the challenge of building his perfect soldier. In the end, the woman had jeopardized the entire program, out of her own weakness. Ouelet had never had a child of her own, and it was clear to him now that she had projected that part of herself onto the Major.

"That's the problem with the human heart," Cutter told Ouelet. He raised his pistol and shot twice through the glass. Both bullets struck Ouelet in the left side of her chest. She lived just long enough to comprehend what had happened. She did not look surprised as she died.

Even at half her normal capacity, the Major was still a match for the best-trained human, and her hard-wired, combat-programmed training was now fully active. She attacked and disarmed the security personnel who crossed her path with ease. Her actions were rote and mechanical, operating on a level that was instinctive, beyond her normal thought processes. It was now simply escape, evade, and survive.

In the Hanka parking garage, the Major found a motorcycle that suited her needs, a fat black Honda with plenty of torque. She jumped onto it and broke open the ignition control with a twist of her fingers, hot-wiring the system. The electric motor hummed to life and she gunned it, lifting herself off the seat and leaning into the handlebars.

The parking lot guard tried to grab her. He caught

the motorcycle's rear frame and was dragged along behind it as the Major sped down the exit ramp. Once she was sure of her balance, she kicked the guard off, and he tumbled into the wall.

The ramp emptied out into the downtown streets of New Port City and the Major turned the bike to blend in with the traffic, soon leaving the tower of Hanka Robotics far behind and out of sight.

11

△

FLASHBACK MEMORY

Aramaki was normally hard to read, but Batou and Togusa, summoned to his office, could tell the chief was extremely unhappy. His words were more curt and clipped than usual, and Cutter was there via hologram, which never improved the mood of anyone in Section Nine. Worse, while Cutter sounded convincing, the story he told didn't jibe with the Major they all knew.

"I want to see her scan," Aramaki told Cutter's hologram.

"She killed Dr. Ouelet!" Cutter exclaimed. Even if that were true, and Batou didn't believe it, they should be allowed to see what had gone wrong with the Major's cerebral enhancements.

But Cutter did not want Section Nine anywhere near the Major. "You're to have no further contact with her," the Hanka CEO stated. "Hanka Security will hunt her from here."

Batou spoke up without asking for permission. "And what are their orders?"

"To terminate on sight." Cutter didn't seem the least bit distressed by the prospect.

"You want to kill her?" Batou exclaimed. "You *built* her!" He moved angrily towards the hologram, as though Cutter were physically in Aramaki's office and could therefore be punched in the face.

Cutter didn't respond, but addressed Aramaki instead. "Have your sergeant stand down."

"The Major would never harm Dr. Ouelet!" Batou said, trying to make the chief see reason.

Togusa put a restraining hand on Batou's arm. "Come on."

"She's not the Major anymore!" Cutter sounded irritated that no one at Section Nine had grasped this. "We have a Section Nine operative under terrorist programming. This goes public, your unit goes down."

So now Cutter was threatening to disband the entire Section Nine department should it prove an embarrassment to Hanka.

Aramaki inhaled, then said, "You kill her, you kill us." Even if the whole business managed to stay secret, Section Nine would fall apart if one of their own were officially murdered. The team wouldn't work for Cutter if he had the Major's blood on his hands. Batou's respect for the chief grew.

"I'll take that under advisement," Cutter said in

a tone of false courtesy. Then his hologram cut out, dissolving into falling fragments of code that glittered before vanishing.

Batou turned to the chief. "So what now?"

Instead of speaking, Aramaki reached behind his desk, opened a drawer and took out an old-fashioned revolver. Its leather holster was embossed with the image of a samurai with his sword raised above his head, about to strike at an enemy.

The Avalon Apartments complex was arranged in a towering set of rings. At one time, the design plan had called for an atrium with majestic trees in the middle of the circular walkways that engirdled each floor, but that notion had fallen by the wayside as the place grew cheaper and dingier. Now it just looked like some kind of giant upended tube. Characterized by crumbling concrete, rusted railings and lines of laundry hanging from windows, the Avalon was home to those who didn't have the means to get themselves off of New Port City's bottom rungs and had reluctantly made their peace with it.

The residents went about their morning, and none of them spotted the lithe female figure loitering in the shadows. None of them saw her fingering the key in her hand, turning over the question of what it might represent in her thoughts.

She entered one of the buildings around the

circular courtyard and took a rattling elevator up to the nineteenth floor. The Major could hear the tenants chatting or watching television through the poorly insulated walls.

On the walkway of the floor below, a mother and her toddler emerged from another elevator. The child said something and the mother answered. Her words were unclear but the affection in her tone wafted up to the Major. A comedian was doing a routine on TV in one of the apartments; his patter brought laughter and applause from his studio audience.

The Major found the apartment door of Unit 1912. She listened for a moment, holding her breath. Now she was here, she found herself frozen in a final moment of indecision. She truthfully had no idea what she would find on the other side of the door. It was ajar, and a cat ran out—a grey-and-black tabby with a blue collar, identical to the one in her glitch. The animal ran straight up to Major, winding around her legs, purring.

Instinctively, she picked up the cat. "Hey, hey."

The tenant of 1912, presumably the cat's owner, came hurrying out of the apartment. "Oh, the, Pum—Pumpkin!" she called to the cat.

Looking down at the walkway, where she expected the cat to be, the elderly woman almost collided with the Major. She was Japanese and looked to be in her sixties, slim, small, and well-kept. There was a proud and weary cast to her face. Unlike most people in the city, who wore muted, neutral colors, Hairi Kusanagi was clad in a stylish, if outdated, dress of deep greens, blues and purples arranged in a print that suggested elements of a folktale. Hairi was startled briefly by the woman holding her cat, but she straightened and smiled. "Oh, you surprised me."

She had a strong Japanese accent, but spoke in English, perhaps assuming that the Caucasian Major might understand her better that way. Pumpkin, nestled in the Major's arms, gave a contented meow. "Ooh," Hairi chuckled, "she likes you."

The Major didn't know exactly how to respond to either the woman's amiable manner or the cat's placid acceptance. For that matter, she didn't know how to explain what she was doing here. She couldn't imagine they had ever met before—that would stretch coincidence to the breaking point—but the impression of the older woman seemed strangely potent, almost *familiar*, and the Major felt a flicker of confusion. Perhaps this woman was somehow famous and the Major had heard of her on the news? She also had an air of contained sorrow underlying her kindness. The Major began speaking before she'd determined what to say. "I was looking... for, um... "

Hairi didn't seem bothered by the stranger on her doorstep. She stuttered occasionally as she spoke. "No, co-come in." She opened the door wider and beckoned. The Major was so surprised that she stood where she was. "No," the older woman said, "come, come. Okay."

The Major, still carrying Pumpkin, followed the woman into the apartment. It was small but neat, with artwork and photos on the wall.

"Okay," Hairi said. She turned to the Major. "Can I offer you some tea?"

"Okay," the Major replied.

The older woman nodded, as though that was the answer she wanted. "Uh-huh." She headed into the kitchen where she lit the burner under the kettle. Unlike the Major's apartment or the homes of the Hanka scientists, this place was thoroughly lived-in. The paint on the kitchen walls was fading, but there were green plants in pots on the sill by the window's wooden frame, hangers on a line that stretched along the ceiling, and colourful mismatched cups on the draining board. In the main room, cheap chairs flanked a square table that held a basket of citrus fruit. Hairi Kusanagi might be old, and she looked like she had regrets, but she clearly had a life.

The Major set Pumpkin down. The cat promptly trotted through the open door of a bedroom. The Major looked inside, curious, and found that everything in the room was draped in plastic, to keep it exactly as it had been, so that neither dust nor the passage of time could harm it. The posters on the wall, the bedspread, the dolls on the shelf, the clothes in the closet all suggested that the room belonged to a teenage girl.

Hairi appeared just behind the Major. "That's Motoko's room."

The Major stiffened at the name of the girl in her glitch visions.

The older woman, as if anticipating a question, said, "My daughter died a year ago."

No wonder Hairi had an air of such grief about her. "I'm sorry," the Major said, meaning it.

"She ran away," Hairi said. "She was difficult. And, uh, we fought." She managed a chuckle at the memory.

The cat was now on the bed, cleaning herself. The animal also seemed familiar to the Major, more familiar even than the glitch visions would explain.

The older woman looked philosophical as she added, "But I guess we all fight with our parents, right?"

The Major looked around and noticed a small bronze pagoda on a shelf in Motoko's room. She stared at it. It, too, seemed very familiar.

"Uh, please come and sit, yeah?" Hairi gestured for the Major to come out of the bedroom and sit at the dining table. The Major sat politely as Hairi retrieved a teapot from the kitchen, then sat across the table from her. All around the living room were framed still photographs. Almost every one included the same young girl, as a child and as a teenager. None of the images showed her past that point, however. The resemblance to Hairi was striking. The girl must be Motoko. If these pictures of her were taken just before her death, she had died young.

The Major wasn't sure how she ought to express her sympathies. She hoped the older woman would speak again. Hairi chuckled softly, but then smiled nervously and looked away.

An awkward silence fell. When it was clear Hairi wasn't going to speak up, the Major did. "What happened to her?"

"Mmm, I don't know." The older woman's chuckle this time was melancholy. "Um, the Ministry sent me her ashes, and they told me she took her own life. But Motoko…" She shook her head with certainty. "Ah, no, no, no." Another chuckle, this one in recognition of the Ministry's falsehood, one so obvious to her that it was bleakly amusing someone had dared to give it as an explanation. "I n-never believed them. Sh-she was *happy*… living in the lawless zone with her friends. She'd write her manifestos about how technology was d-destroying the world. Oh, then one day the police came… and they ran." She paused. "It's strange."

In the kitchen, the kettle started to whistle. Hairi went to turn the burner off, continuing, "I see her in so many young women. On the street, in my dreams." She returned from the kitchen with the kettle in hand, pouring water into the teapot, "As if she's still here." She sighed, fond nostalgia coloring her speech. "Ah, she was fearless! A-and wild. You remind me of her." The nervous chuckle came again. "Sorry."

The Major stood up. This was all very strange. "How do I remind you of her?"

"The way you look at me," the woman told her. There was strong emotion in her tone and in her gaze, but there was curiosity as well. "Who *are* you?" she asked.

"I don't know." It was an admission of despair. The Major suddenly could not bear to be here any longer. She did not know where to go next, or what to do with what she had found, but she felt she had to go at once.

"Wait, wait," Hairi called before the Major could reach the door. "Wait!"

The Major stopped and turned to face her.

"Will you come again to visit me?" the woman asked, hope in her voice.

The Major was flooded with contradictory emotions—she felt that she would come apart if she remained any longer, and yet she also felt a pang at leaving. "I will," she promised, and then left before Hairi could see the tears falling from her eyes.

Aramaki sat at his desk in the semi-darkness of his office, loading bullets into his old-fashioned revolver.

Most of Section Nine had been deployed on individual search and sweep investigations, scouring the city for any sign of Major Mira Killian. A report from a police drone had turned up a possible sighting in the lower city, but it was a dead end. Aramaki was not surprised. The Major was one of the best operatives he had ever worked with, and he knew that if she wanted to vanish into the metropolitan sprawl and go unseen, then there was little they could do to find her. With a conventional fugitive, Aramaki could count on them, sooner or later, to make a mistake or overlook a crucial detail. The Major, on the other hand, simply wasn't wired that way.

But he knew her well. He knew that she would not disappear, not like this. Not without making things clear first.

When she made contact, he was waiting for it.

"*Aramaki.*" The chief's name echoed through the ghostly pseudo-telepathic space of the mind-comms link. The Major was walking on the bridge heading away from the apartment complex, her black coat flapping in the cold wind. It hadn't started to rain yet, but thunderclouds were piling atop one another in the sky. "*Listen to me. I was never in a terrorist bombing. My parents... everything was data they installed in my mind.*" She took a breath. "*And there were others. Runaways like me... considered disposable. Kuze was one of them. That's why he's coming. For Hanka.*"

Aramaki rose and leant on his desk, forming the words sub-vocally to be transmitted into his encrypted neural implant. "*Can you prove this?*" Aramaki asked into the comm.

"*Dr. Ouelet can,*" the Major replied.

Aramaki was blunt. "*Ouelet's dead.*"

The Major was too stunned to respond. Despite everything, Genevieve Ouelet had known the Major as she was now better than anyone alive, and she had saved her life in the end. The Major had thought Ouelet might get into trouble for engineering the escape, but she was sure the doctor was far too valuable to Hanka for her to be too severely punished.

Aramaki broke into her reverie. "*Cutter says you killed her.*"

She knew that Cutter was behind everything, behind the deaths of the runaways, the theft of the Major's true identity, and now this. The Major told Aramaki, "*Put me on the grid.*" If she showed up on the computer networks, the help she needed would come to her. "*I need Kuze to find me.*"

Aramaki walked to his office door, put on his overcoat and picked up his briefcase. His two assistants opened the office double doors to facilitate his exit. "*Cutter will see you, too,*" he told the Major.

"*I know,*" the Major replied over the comm. "*But I need to do this.*"

Cutter was already monitoring the conversation from his office, listening in on the Major and Aramaki through a surveillance cable he had plugged into his quik-port. He was not surprised that the unstable Major would seek out the even more unstable terrorist Kuze, but he was disappointed in Aramaki. Cutter had always believed that the old man put duty above all else. Of course, Aramaki might see his duty as being dictated by a certain version of the facts, but Hanka was the underpinning of everything in this country. His loyalty should be to his employer, the corporation, even when that meant embracing changes. Since it wasn't he would have to go too.

"*I'm going to meet with the prime minister,*" Aramaki told the Major over the comm. "*Cutter will be held responsible for what he has done. He must be stopped.*"

The conversation ended and Cutter removed the monitoring cable from his quik-port. He sighed and said aloud, "The virus has spread."

Aramaki's beat-up brown sedan was in its usual space in the open-air parking lot next to the building where the Section Nine office was housed. Someone of his rank could have easily requisitioned a new model, even a limousine with a driver, but Aramaki hated ostentation, and he hated waste even more. The engine was still in top shape. Also, he had found that driving alone was an excellent way to clear his mind so that he could concentrate on what mattered most.

He got into the driver's seat, briefcase still in hand, and reached out to the Section Nine team over his mind-comm. He had little doubt that the link was no longer secure, but he had to risk making contact. Batou, Togusa and the others had to be warned. "*All agents switch to mind-comms, now!*" Tense, he shifted his briefcase to his right side as he awaited a response.

Before a reply had time to reach Aramaki, the passenger window blew inward, shards of glass flying. A team of three assassins, each wearing a black military jacket and dark trousers, faces hidden behind full tactical masks, opened fire on the chief's car with machine guns. Aramaki slid to the floor, holding his briefcase above his head. The assassins completely riddled the vehicle with bullets.

When the machine guns at last stopped chattering and the car had more punctures than intact metal, the leader of the assassins took out his pistol and approached the vehicle. No one could have survived the barrage of gunfire, but it was necessary to check. The assassin reached for the door handle—

The door flew open, slamming the assassin in the head. Aramaki could hear the man scream from beneath his mask. He emerged from his ruined car, completely unharmed, and fired his old .357 Magnum at the assassin. The revolver was virtually an antique in this modern era, but it still possessed incredible stopping power—and at close range it shredded the assassin's body armor, blasting him back off his feet and into a heap.

Aramaki had been put in command of Section Nine because of his clear strategic thinking, uncompromising work ethic and his seniority. Contrary to what people like Cutter might have thought, the chief had not been taken out of the field due to any fading of his abilities; age had not diminished him in the least.

Now he used his considerable marksmanship and

experience to employ his briefcase as a shield while the two remaining assassins fired at him. Aramaki aimed at the second shooter, who was still reacting to the thunderous reports of the old Magnum. The second assassin fell.

Catching sight of his target, the third assassin opened fire, bullets clanking into the flank of the parked car. This time, Aramaki landed an aimed shot in the shooter's chest, dropping him to his knees.

The first man he'd shot was still alive and trying to get away across the asphalt, coughing up blood and retching as he crawled. Aramaki kicked him over onto his back, as one might flip over a cockroach, and gazed at the wounded man with something almost, but not quite, like pity. "Don't send a rabbit to kill a fox," he advised. Then Aramaki shot the assassin in the head.

He snapped open the revolver's cylinder and let the spent brass shell casings fall from his gun onto the dead assassin's chest, then started walking at a casual pace toward the sidewalk. "*We are burned,*" he warned his team over the mind-comm. It wouldn't count for much in a frontal assault, but at least they'd know not to walk into a Hanka trap and they'd know not to reveal anything over the comms that they didn't want Cutter to hear. "*I repeat. We are burned.*"

Batou sat on the rooftop of the apartment building where he lived, enjoying the feel of the cool night air on his skin and the high view of the city around him. He'd brought the basset hound mix Gabriel home with him, and now the dog was thumping his tail at Batou's side—until the dog smelled trouble and whined.

"Shh," he told the dog. He could sense the approaching hitmen as well, but didn't want them to know it before he was ready. Batou's pistol was concealed in his lap.

Togusa was eating dinner in a noodle shop. He glanced up at an overhead mirror, reaching for a concealed weapon at his waist as he saw the reflection of an armed man coming up behind him. Suddenly he twisted in his seat and shot the gunman, then pivoted and shot another. Finally he leapt to his feet and shot a third approaching from directly ahead of him, a feat that gave him pride but scared the hell out of passing pedestrians, who scattered in shrieking panic. Togusa leant against a wall and emitted a sigh of relief.

Having taken care of the cadre on the rooftop, Batou pushed his car to its limits, stripping gears and sending other drivers spinning out of his way as he raced through the night.

In a place of safety, Kuze lay still while a geisha bot tended to his repairs, each of her actions controlled by his commands. He could simply have remained here forever, but even though he and the bot were similar in their physical composition, they were not the same. She did not have a ghost as he did, and that loneliness had become more than he could bear.

The Major was on a different road, back on the motorcycle she'd stolen from the Hanka parking lot. A billboard floated past her with the legend NIVOZEN." She headed for the ramp labeled CENTRAL.

"Mr. Cutter." The operative's voice reached Cutter over the comm. He was in a Zen garden on the rooftop of Hanka. It was a place of peace, with large green plants and a rectangular lily pond. He summoned a large hologram that showed him the entire city, but he saw no need to be tense while observing the endgame from this safe distance. "We've located the Major on the grid," the operative reported. "She's in the lawless zone. Air support five minutes out."

"Is the spider tank within range?" Cutter inquired into the comm. He manipulated the hologram so that it zeroed in on one section, now displaying in detail a large plaza in the lawless zone. In the plaza's center was the pagoda from the Major's visions, as well as a large banyan tree. Cutter sat on a garden bench facing the hologram, settling in for his inevitable victory.

"Yes, sir," the operative replied over the comm. "Awaiting your orders, sir."

The Major dismounted the motorcycle in the plaza. The place appeared to be completely abandoned, and had been that way for some time. She remembered what it had looked like, though. She wandered over the broken pavement until she came to the charred remnants of the pagoda, nestled in the roots of the banyan tree that had kept growing despite the fire damage. A flock of pigeons took wing at her approach, startled by the active life continuing amidst the destruction.

Another glitch unfolded as the Major looked up, though this one was both longer and much smoother than the ones that had come before. In it, a blinding searchlight shone down on the pagoda from a hycop. An officer in charge issued stern warnings through his megaphone. Flames were engulfing the little building. The soldiers who had set the fire were everywhere, rounding up the adolescents who had made their home in the pagoda. The teens were all yelling in anger and terror as they were being hauled out of the burning dwelling, then beaten to the ground. And Cutter had been there, standing to one side, keeping his expensive shirtcuffs and shoes clean as he watched the raid unfold.

The officer issued another warning. The girl Motoko sobbed and screamed as she was torn from Hideo's arms, despite all his efforts to hold onto her.

"Motoko!" Hideo cried. Their voices echoed in the Major's memory. Hideo's despairing screams became harder to hear as he was dragged away in the other direction, but a soldier pulled Motoko along, straight toward the Major.

The elements of the glitch vanished one by one—the soldiers, the pagoda, the other teenagers, Hideo—until only Motoko remained. When the vision of Motoko reached her, it was as if the two figures—machine and girl—were merging. Then Motoko vanished as well, leaving the Major alone in the plaza.

She took a moment, then entered what was left of the pagoda. Around her were what remained of the runaways' squat. Plant life had sprung up from the ashes, spreading green tendrils through the blackened remnants of the wooden-slat walls. The fire had spared a mosaic, some keys that had been made into a display and some handprints in the plaster along one wall. The Major reached out her own hand to stroke the prints, all that was left of the young people who had banded together and made a home here.

An electronic voice with a buzzing echo spoke up behind her. "It is real," Kuze said. He entered the pagoda and stood behind the Major. He sounded more than a little awed. "This place."

"I remember what they did to us," the Major told him. "Cutter and his men. This is where they took us from." She walked over to a niche and gestured at the ground where their bedrolls had been. "We used to sleep right here. We were like a family. All of us runaways. We had nothing... except each other. They took that from us." Her voice was soft and bitter.

She saw some graffiti carved into the niche, names of some of those who'd stayed here: Minori, Hideo, Motoko, Miya, Reika. And now she knew who Kuze was. "Your name was Hideo."

Kuze looked up, and spoke the Major's real name. "Motoko."

She couldn't speak. For the second time that day, tears welled in her eyes.

"That was your name," Kuze said tenderly. He approached her, and said her name again. "Motoko."

They gazed at each other, memories overlapping who they were now. The Major wondered who they would be if they had been allowed to live their lives together uninterrupted. Hideo had wanted to be an artist, Motoko had aspired to be a poet, both bringing beauty to the world. Instead, they had been transformed. Vengeance, death, destruction. This was the art they made now.

"Come with me... into my network," Kuze urged. The Major looked at him, not sure what he meant. "We will evolve beyond them. And together we can avenge what they have done to us." His electronic voice buzzed. "Come... with me." He was proposing that they exist together in a purely cyber world, from where they could strike out at humanity.

Before the Major could answer, a mortar blast hit the pagoda, hurling both the Major and Kuze out into the plaza. She hit hard and stayed down, while he bounced, sustaining greater injuries on his second landing.

In the Zen garden, Cutter wielded a virtual remote control, directing the real arsenal he had in place in the lawless zone. He watched the spider tank's slow and steady advance. So much raw power, and it responded from so far away to his every gesture. This, truly, was the pinnacle of human achievement.

"I'll take control from here," he told his soldiers over the comm. The intricate hologram of the spider tank glowed red, at odds with the peace of the garden.

"Weapons system manual command," the female operative's voice confirmed. "Spider tank now active."

The Major lay on her front. Parts of her artificial skin had been obliterated in the blast, leaving her inner workings open to the night air. A tremor went through the road, echoing up through her boots, followed by another and another. Turning toward the source, she looked up and saw something that seemed to have crawled out of a nightmare, a gigantic tank that scrabbled and stomped forward on six huge metal segmented legs, red triangular lights glowing above its turret gun like enraged eyes, motors grinding as it swung its turret around, tracking her. Pistons hissed as it moved and the machine began to advance on the plaza.

The Major got to her feet and ran to Kuze. Like her, he had been damaged by the mortar. Both of his legs were shattered. All that remained under his left thigh was part of a metal pole, which, until this attack, had been encased in sensors, artificial muscles and cyber-flesh.

"It's Cutter! He's found us!" The Major grabbed Kuze as the tank started firing. Its ordnance was not machine bullets, but explosive missiles three feet in length.

The Major dragged Kuze as quickly as she could into the cover provided by the banyan tree's thick roots, then ran to her motorcycle and grabbed a machine gun from where she'd stashed it.

She darted out from cover so she could get a better shot at the gargantuan metal spider that spit bombs instead of poison. Another *whoosh* signaled a second incoming rocket. The Major rolled to evade the blast in time, taking cover behind one of the pillars supporting the walkway overhead that engirdled the plaza.

Shrapnel ricocheted off the stonework and the concrete pillar. The Major felt a razor of torn steel clip her arm, but she ignored it.

The tank continued to fire. The hologram wasn't showing Cutter the Major's present position, but that was all right. Time was on his side. He would, if necessary, raze the entire plaza until no two bits of concrete larger than his thumb remained intact and nothing organic or inorganic survived.

Cutter turned the tank's muzzle toward the banyan tree where Kuze was concealed. The Major leapt away from her own hiding place to draw his aim away. She fired at the monstrous arachnid weapon, then ducked back behind the column as the tank blasted at her again.

The next rocket looped down at her, tracking her thermal signature, and slammed into the column. Concrete splintered as the pillar broke apart halfway up its length. Suddenly robbed of any support, a section of the elevated pedestrian pathway collapsed, smashing into pieces amid a cloud of choking grey dust. The spider tank maintained its barrage, destroying one pillar after another. The pedestrian bridge collapsed section by section.

The Major jumped onto the bridge, keeping ahead of its fall, and used it as a launch to get herself to the plaza's second-story balcony. She took cover behind a V-shaped post. The tank's next blast missed her body, but it blew the gun out of her hand, wounding her arm. She had to find a different approach, circle around, and get closer to the tank. If she couldn't find a way to defeat the machine, this fight would be over in moments.

She sidled over into the shadows cast by what

remained of the bridge so that she was more fully concealed, then inspected the damage in her arm. There was no time to do anything about it—the tank was again marching toward the banyan tree, closing in on Kuze's position. The Major lunged out, seized her gun from where it had fallen, and began to reload.

Below her, the tank finally found Kuze. The machine aimed its multiple guns directly at his head. Kuze, ever defiant, pointed his finger as if it were a gun back at the tank and pretended to shoot. Cutter smiled at the futile gesture.

The Major sprang out into the open and fired at the spider tank. The tank turned from Kuze to resume its assault on the Major. She ran along the balcony, keeping ahead of it as the tank spun, exchanging fire with her as both of them moved.

Cutter watched the thermographic outline of the Major as it flashed between the cover of the pillars. He couldn't figure out what she hoped to achieve. There was no way out now, surely she understood that.

The spider tank extended the scope for its mortar cannon and locked onto the Major. Over the tank's speaker, a female voice announced, "Target acquired."

The spider tank fired a missile at the Major, hitting the balcony. A second hit caused the balcony to collapse.

"No!" Kuze shouted. The single word echoed into the night.

The female voice announced placidly, "Target eliminated."

Cutter exhaled in satisfaction. No experiment had ever been so vexing in its results, or so hard to eradicate, but now he and Hanka were done with 2571. The only task remaining was to get rid of Kuze. Using his VR control, Cutter aimed the spider tank. When Hanka had disposed of that failed prototype, even though it was in pieces, they should have made sure it was truly extinguished; they should never have assumed the Kuze iteration of the project would fail on its own and become inert. Instead, it had literally, if imperfectly, rebuilt itself and very nearly brought down the entire corporation out of an implacable need for vengeance. It was a mistake Cutter would ensure was never made on future projects. Although Kuze could not hear him, the Hanka CEO conceded, "You came close, you freak."

Cutter manipulated the holographic controls, which caused a claw to extend from the spider tank. The huge mechanical appendage seized Kuze by the head, lifted him into the air and pressed him against the banyan tree's trunk, where it began to crush him.

Kuze trembled as his cybernetic systems struggled through a kind of pain-shock, teetering on the edge of shutting down.

This would be death then, he thought. *True death, not the moment of flawed rebirth that has made me what I am now.* Regret washed over him. He would perish never knowing the full truth of who he had been. But at least he had found *her* before it had come to this.

The Major, the thermoptics on her suit engaged, rippled transparently in the light cast by the fires still burning from the explosions. She ran out from the rubble behind the tank and leapt up onto the back of the massive spider. As she landed, the thermoptics in her suit disengaged, leaving her fully visible again. The turret ground its gears and swiveled as the remote operator attempted to unseat the Major, but she was already moving.

She tried firing at the tank's motor center, but there was no result whatsoever. The Major abandoned that tactic and tossed her gun aside. She crawled closer to the motor center. She knew how this tank was powered, whether from real experience or from the implantation of someone else's memories, it didn't matter now. She tried punching it repeatedly with her good fist. Then she grabbed the motor center with both hands and began pulling up on it with all her cyber-augmented strength, howling from the effort.

A camera rose from the tank's upper regions to relay images of this attack back to Cutter. At first, he thought the Major had simply lost her mind. She had been built to be powerful, but she was no match for the components of the spider tank.

And then the operative's voice informed him, "Motor center compromised."

As Cutter watched with disbelief that became

wrath, the Major continued to pull on the tank's central power source.

Inside the Major's eyes, a train of red warning icons cascaded down the side of her vision, malfunction alerts from the hits she had taken from the auto-cannon and the falling rubble. This would take all her remaining strength, and even then there was no guarantee that would be enough.

The usually invisible connections on her joints and epidermis began to reveal themselves and then come apart, a blue light from her core glowing through them. She felt the tank shudder and buck, trying to throw her off as it stumbled in a half-circle on sparking legs. Her fingers bit into the edges of motor casing and she felt it shift, dislodging but still not fully disconnected.

Redoubling her exertion, the Major gripped the armored casing and strained with all her might as the warning grew louder. Actuators and synthetic muscles in her arms went past the red line and beyond all tolerances, stressed to breaking point as the motor center creaked and distorted.

Then, with a sudden screeching crackle of breaking metal, the motor center ripped away from the tank. The force of the action was so powerful that the Major's left forearm came off with the motor, jetting white fluid.

With nothing to power it, the tank's pincers released Kuze, who slid to the ground just before the motor center exploded, enveloping Major in the resultant fireball. The tank gave a shuddering groan and shut down, its six segmented legs trapped beneath it as it collapsed against the stonework of the plaza. Unable to arrest her fall, the Major's ruined body rolled down the face of the machine and clattered to the ground.

Her cyborg frame was a mess of critical damage, half-destroyed, shot through by heavy-caliber bullets and shrapnel. Pale silicate liquid pooled around her head in a shimmering white halo.

Kuze managed to extricate himself from the banyan tree's roots. She watched as he slowly dragged himself over. He collapsed onto the ground next to her.

Both the Major and Kuze appeared near death, but Cutter was done underestimating his enemies. "Sniper team on site?" he asked into the comm.

The sniper team's hycop was en route to the lawless zone. The door opened so that the two snipers could scope out their prey and ready their long-range gun, a weapon so large that it took two of them to wield it effectively.

"We're approaching the targets now, sir," the lead sniper replied into his comm.

Kuze lay beside the Major. "Come with me." His voice was an echoing wheeze now, but his determination was as clear as it had ever been. There was an ugly gouge in his skull trickling with sparks. Despite the terrible, damage that had been done to him, he seemed almost *serene*. "There is no place for us here."

She understood what he was offering. They could be together as they had been, Motoko and Hideo, escaping into the virtual so that no one could ever harm them, ever find them, because no one would know they were there. In their own world, they would be together and whole, and they could bend reality to whatever they wanted it to be, and it would last as long as they wanted it to last. No more lies, no more fighting, because there would be no one who needed her protection.

"No." She hoped he could understand. "I'm not ready to leave." She inhaled deeply, taking in as much of the night air as her bruised lungs would accept. "I belong here."

Kuze looked at her with love. He would not force her, so instead he told her, "I will always be there with you... in your ghost." Then the light went out in Kuze's eyes and his consciousness fled.

Above, the snipers in the hycop took aim. "Target is in view," the lead sniper said into the comm.

"What are you waiting for?" Cutter snapped. "Do it!"

The snipers fired the long-range gun. The shot hit Kuze's head, destroying the human brain within.

"No!" the Major screamed. They couldn't do this—he had wanted his ghost to continue, but now...

"Keep firing," Cutter ordered into the comm.

* * *

Aramaki walked through the corridor of an expensively carpeted building, speaking over his mind-comm. *"Saito, have you found Major? Is she safe?"*

Saito, the best long-distance shot in the unit, lay on his belly on a rooftop. He had eyes on the Major. A sniper's rifle was in his hands and he had an excellent view of both the lawless zone's plaza and the hycop hovering above it. *"She will be,"* Saito told the chief over the mind-comm.

He fired a shot directly into the hycop's rotor. The hycop spun out of control, crashing down to the plaza in a fireball that sent up chunks of the aircraft and rubble in equal measure. Saito ducked back behind the roof's raised edge to avoid being hit by shrapnel, but had to admit to himself that it was quite a rush to bring down something so large and deadly with a single bullet.

Batou walked out of the darkness to the semi-conscious Major and lifted her into his lap. "Hey." He examined her. She looked godawful. Anybody else would die of such injuries, but the Major was the toughest person he knew. "Hey," he repeated.

The Major turned her head to look up at him.

At least she was conscious. "Hey," Batou said once more by way of greeting.

After thinking it over, the Major spoke. "Say

something nice." Repeating what Batou had told her back when she'd first seen his artificial eyes.

Instead of commenting on the ghastly injuries she'd sustained, Batou asked, "What's your name? Aramaki told me you had a name… from before."

"Motoko," the Major confided. Her breathing was very weak.

Batou hoped she still identified as the compatriot he knew, the one he would gladly fight beside and die for. He didn't try to hide his emotion. "Major is still in there, right?"

"I am," the Major assured him.

He sighed in relief. All around them, the lawless zone burned, flames shooting and spreading in the wreckage and rubble. One of the hycop's rotors had half-buried itself in the concrete, sticking up like a giant shark fin, a warning to any who might venture near.

Batou helped her to her feet. They stood looking at one another. The Major put her hand on Batou's chest. Life wasn't just about what had happened in the past. It was the people who were here for her now, and Batou was foremost among them.

The corridor led Aramaki to an elevator, which opened onto the Hanka building's rooftop garden. No one was expecting the old man who ran Section Nine to show up, and before Cutter's guards could consider what Aramaki might be doing there, he shot and killed them all.

Cutter's horror at the Major's survival was so absolute that at first he did not even react to the sound of nearby gunfire. Then he saw Aramaki approaching and deactivated the hologram of the plaza. The Hanka CEO had no wish to gaze on the visual report of his defeat any longer.

"Mr. Cutter." Aramaki's tone was formal. "I've come from the prime minister. You are charged with murder and crimes against the state."

Cutter turned and started walking away around the rectangular perimeter of the lily pond. Aramaki followed, so the two men were circling each other.

The CEO had guessed that, if it came down to it, Aramaki would be the one to arrest him. "I thought that it might be you." At least, Aramaki would be the one to *try* to arrest him.

Aramaki knew what Cutter would do next, but felt obliged to warn him against it. "It is unwise to resist."

Cutter abruptly reached for his gun. It was a much more modern, sleek weapon, but Aramaki was much faster with his .357 and shot Cutter before he could fire. The defeated man dropped to the ground.

Aramaki walked over to the Hanka executive and kicked the gun out of his reach. His wound painful but not fatal, Cutter struggled to his feet and held his arms up in surrender. He was frightened now, whimpering, "Please." After everything he had done, all the lives he had taken, Cutter didn't want to die.

"*Major?*" Aramaki spoke into his comm.

In the plaza, the Major had some of her weight on Batou, but was managing to walk under her own power. "*I'm with Cutter,*" Aramaki announced into the mind-comm. Now that the moment of truth was here, he could only be its instrument. "*Is there anything you'd like to say to him?*"

Her reply came back to him over the wireless digital network, and he sensed her out there in the aftermath of the battle, broken but unbowed. "*Tell him this is justice,*" the Major replied. "*It's what I was built for.*" She had been made to kill terrorists, and Cutter had proved himself to be the worst of them all.

"*So,*" Aramaki asked her, "*do I have your consent?*"

Despite her injuries, the Major stood straight. Whatever Hideo Kuze had hoped for her, she could never return to being who she had been, and Mira Killian was an illusion, constructed from falsehoods. And yet she was real, and she had a place in this world. "*My name is Major, and I give my consent.*"

Aramaki shot Cutter through the heart. He fell back into the lily pond, unable to keep his head from being submerged. His last sensation was of falling into dark water, just like the false memory he'd had implanted into the woman who had once been Motoko Kusanagi.

EPILOGUE

RISE

The city graveyard was very large, and all of the tombstones were similar, flat and gray, set in concentric rings of likewise gray cement walkways. It took some time for the Major to find the grave she was seeking. Eventually, she located it, helped by the fresh lilies that had been placed there not long ago. The inscription read: MOTOKO KUSANAGI. She knelt over it, reflecting. There were things she wanted to say to the girl she had been, and to the warrior she was still in the process of becoming.

She had a sense she was being watched, and turned to see Motoko's mother Hairi Kusanagi. It was she who had put the flowers on the grave, but now the elderly woman hung back at a respectful distance.

The Major stood, making her way past the stone memorials until she reached Hairi. The two women looked tenderly into one another's eyes. "You don't have to come here anymore," the Major said. Motoko's body was gone, but her mind and spirit, her ghost, were right here, in front of her mother.

Hairi nodded. "I know." Trembling with joy, she embraced her daughter.

The Major gasped, realizing that Hairi had recognized her even at the apartment. No matter that Motoko was in a new form; Hairi had her child back and there was nothing that could matter more.

She smiled and hugged Hairi in return.

"Yes," Hairi whispered.

The Major exhaled into her mother's shoulder, fully contented for the first time since she had been placed in the shell.

Later, Hairi set about restoring her apartment. Bustling with excitement, she removed the plastic from Motoko's bed and the furniture in the room, readying it for the Major's next visit. She knew that the Major was too old to play with dolls, of course, but Hairi left them there on the shelf. The toys had made Motoko very happy, and Hairi hoped that seeing the dolls might bring the Major happy memories. Whatever she did, whatever she looked like, whatever name she had, the Major was Hairi's child, and she was alive. That last fact was enough to make Hairi feel that she, too, had been reborn.

The Section Nine team disembarked from a helicopter on a downtown skyscraper roof. The Major stood on the roof of an adjoining tower and let the wind wash over her, gently pulling her this way and that. She turned her face into the breeze. It ruffled her dark hair, and chilled her flawless, unmarked skin.

In the reflection off the silver and gold mirror of the building across from her, she saw herself—a lithe figure under a dark overcoat, watchful and waiting. She was whole and restored, her body renewed, improved... and somehow, more *human* than it had ever been before.

Holographic billboards floated between the rooftops, but the Major paid the ads no mind. They were only clutter for those who were easily distracted. She settled low into a crouch, her cybernetic eyes never blinking, taking in everything as she waited for the command to move, contemplating the knowledge that had settled on her in the cemetery.

My mind is human. My body is manufactured. I'm the first of my kind, but I won't be the last. We cling to memories as if they define us. But what we do defines us. My ghost survived to remind the next

*of us that humanity is our virtue. I know who I am...
and what I'm here to do.*

As Aramaki entered the building that housed his
office, something different happened. Instead of going
about their usual morning business, every single
person on the floor stood to attention and saluted
him. He acknowledged this with a curt nod, then
spoke over the mind-comm, interrupting the Major's
reverie. "*Major. Engage targets.*"

The Major removed her black coat, readying
the thermoptic bodysuit underneath. She propelled
herself off the roof in a graceful backward dive,
preparing to attack the threat below. They would not
be anticipating an assault from above.

In his office, Aramaki added into the mind-comm,
"*You're authorized.*"

The Major activated the suit's thermoptic aspect,
and she became a shimmer in the air. She was entirely
alive, and she knew exactly who she was.

ABOUT THE AUTHORS

JAMES SWALLOW is a *New York Times* and *Sunday Times* bestseller, the author of over forty-five books, including *Nomad,* the Scribe award winner *Day of the Vipers, The Poisoned Chalice, Nemesis, The Flight of the Eisenstein, Jade Dragon,* the *Sundowners* series of steampunk Westerns, *The Butterfly Effect* and fiction from the worlds of *24, Deus Ex, Star Trek, Judge Dredd, Doctor Who, Stargate* and *Warhammer 40,000.*

Swallow's other credits include the critically acclaimed nonfiction work *Dark Eye: The Films of David Fincher* and scriptwriting for television, video games and audio dramas.

He lives in London, and is currently working on his next book.

ABBIE BERNSTEIN is a native of Los Angeles. Her nonfiction books include *The DNA of Orphan Black*, *The Great Wall: The Art of the Film* and *The Art of Mad Max: Fury Road*. She has also written and directed multiple short films, including *Inconvenience*, *The Rumpelstiltskin Incident* and *The Next Word*, and directed the three-hour documentary *The Making of Robin of Sherwood*.

For more fantastic fiction, author events, exclusive excerpts,
competitions, limited editions and more

VISIT OUR WEBSITE
titanbooks.com

LIKE US ON FACEBOOK
facebook.com/titanbooks

FOLLOW US ON TWITTER
@TitanBooks

EMAIL US
readerfeedback@titanemail.com